**The Gunsmith had fitted his key into the lock when he heard something from inside the room . . .**

Never hesitating, he turned the key with his left hand, and entered the room with his right hand near his gun.

He spotted someone by the window, silhouetted by the moonlight, and made the near fatal mistake of assuming he was alone. By the time he realized his error, a man who had been behind the door stepped out and wrapped powerful arms around him in a bear hug.

Arms pinned at his side, Clint was unable to reach his gun.

**Don't miss any of the lusty, hard-riding action in
the Charter Western series, THE GUNSMITH**

**And coming next month:
The Gunsmith #54: HELL ON WHEELS**

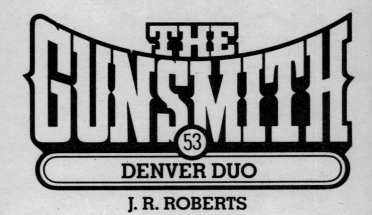

# THE GUNSMITH

## 53

### DENVER DUO

## J. R. ROBERTS

CHARTER BOOKS, NEW YORK

THE GUNSMITH #53: DENVER DUO

A Charter Book / published by arrangement with
the author

PRINTING HISTORY
Charter edition/May 1986

ISBN: 0-441-30957-7

Charter Books are published by The Berkley Publishing Group,
200 Madison Avenue, New York, New York 10016.
PRINTED IN THE UNITED STATES OF AMERICA

To Anna, Christopher and Matthew

# ONE

Because Clint Adams had been to New York, New Orleans, and San Francisco, he decided to go to Denver, a city he had never visited. Although it didn't quite have the ambiance of those other cities, it was considerably larger and busier than most of the western towns he'd been to.

His arrival in Denver had been quiet, for which he was grateful. He had been there a week and still no one had approached him and asked whether he was the notorious Gunsmith. He had, however, seen those old dime novels about the Gunsmith that had been written by J.T. Archer, using a pseudonym, in several bookstores, but he was pleased that there weren't any new ones to be found. His trip to New York some months before had been a success, then. True, he'd discovered that J.T., whom he had met years earlier in Leadtown, had been murdered, and he'd helped to find her killer, but he'd also made sure that no one else would be writing fiction disguised as fact about him. He had enough problems without some writer making him seem bigger than life. The problem with seeming larger than life was that there was always someone else who desired that status and thought that the way to achieve it was to kill someone who already had that grand reputation.

His rig was back in Labyrinth, Texas, because that's where he had been when he decided to take a trip to Denver—for a vacation, as his friend Rick Hartman had put it. Duke was in one of Denver's fine livery stables, and Clint Adams himself was in a fine room at the Denver House Hotel.

And on his seventh morning in Denver, he wasn't alone.

The woman's name was Luisa Crowley, and she was one of those long-legged, classy blondes Clint didn't particularly like, but certainly didn't mind sampling from time to time.

She rolled over, opened her eyes, and found him gazing down at her.

"What are you looking at?" she asked.

"You."

"Why?"

"I'm sorry you're leaving today." He was lying, but he knew she'd be pleased to hear him say it.

"That's sweet," she said, running the forefinger of her right hand along his jaw, "but I must. My husband is expecting me back by tonight."

Clint hadn't known that she was married, and it annoyed him to find out that she was and hadn't told him about it earlier. If he could avoid it, he preferred not to sleep with married women.

"I'm sorry I didn't tell you last night," she said, reading his face, "but things were going so well and I didn't want to ruin them. You don't hate me, do you?"

"No," Clint said, "I don't hate you, Luisa."

He threw the covers back and swung his feet to the floor to start to rise.

"Wait," she said, grabbing his arm. "Where are you going? Can't we . . . say good-bye?"

"We are, Luisa," Clint said, pulling his arm away gently and rising.

"You are angry with me because I'm married."

"Not because you're married," he said. "Because you didn't tell me."

"Would it have made a difference?"

"I can't say, but last night I didn't know you were married, and this morning I do," he explained. "Now, it makes a difference."

"I'm sorry," she said again.

"So am I."

She stood up and said, "I'll get dressed and leave . . . if you really want me to."

She was naked and she was holding her already considerably flat tummy in, so that her small, well-rounded breasts were thrust out. She did have delicious breasts, he thought, looking at her, but he found that he had no desire to sample them once again before she left.

"I really want you to," he said. She frowned, suffering the rejection, and dressed as he silently watched. He didn't want to touch her again, but he didn't mind watching.

When she had her evening gown on again—not looking quite as neat and proper as she had last night—she said, "I don't regret this one bit, Clint."

He said nothing to that. She left, not bothering to try to kiss him good-bye.

He slammed the door angrily. He had enjoyed Denver for six days, even though he'd been unable to find suitable companionship, and when Luisa Crowley had come along— lovely and willing—he'd grabbed her with both hands.

Maybe he should have asked her if she was married, but if he had she might have lied, and if he'd discovered the lie . . .

Don't play it so high and mighty, Adams, he told himself. He decided to dress and go down to have one of Denver House's marvelous breakfasts.

From now until the end of his stay in Denver, he'd be more careful about the female companionship he chose, no matter how long he had to go without.

Clint gave his order to the waiter—the same waiter who had taken care of him since his day of arrival—and asked the man if he could bring him a newspaper with his first pot of coffee. The man, mindful of the generous tips he'd been receiving, said it would be his pleasure.

The coffee was excellent, as usual, but the *Denver Express* headline was something less than usual.

### GRUESOME MURDER OF POLITICIAN'S WIFE IN HOTEL ROOM!

The story explained that a prominent Denver politician's wife had been discovered murdered in a Denver hotel and with her had been a prominent women's suffrage leader's husband. There was no mistaking what they had been doing there, for they were both naked and in bed . . . And dead.

They had each been stabbed numerous times and were positioned on the bed so that the woman's head was in the man's lap.

"Frightening, isn't it?" the waiter inquired.

His voice broke into Clint's concentration and he looked up to see the man standing there with his breakfast plates balanced up and down his arm.

"Yes, it is," Clint said, folding the newspaper and putting it down.

"I don't know what this city's coming to," the man said, putting plates down in front of Clint. The breakfast consisted of scrambled eggs, potatoes, ham, biscuits, jam, and another pot of coffee.

"For that matter," the man went on, "I don't know what

this country is coming to. Do you know that in this same paper, in the center, they are printing excerpts of one of those horrible dime novels? You know, the ones that make heroes out of villains and murderers?''

''Is that a fact?''

''Enjoy your breakfast, Mr. Adams,'' the man said, shaking his head as he walked away.

As the waiter left, Clint picked up the paper again, turned to the center section, and saw that the excerpt was from a dime novel about Wild Bill Hickok, who had been his best friend while he was alive. He did not become angry at seeing the cheap novel because he knew that many of the lies told in the dime novels about Hickok had originated from Hickok himself.

Satisfied that the excerpt was not about him, he directed his attention to his breakfast, reminding himself to go back and finish reading the other article later on.

# TWO

Across town, while Clint Adams ate his breakfast, Ellie Lennox and Amanda Foxworth almost came to blows.

The two women were physically and temperamentally opposite and had only one thing in common. Both of them were Pinkerton operatives.

Pinkerton was not crazy about women detectives, but as an intelligent man he recognized the need—however occasional—for them.

On this particular day Amanda had been called into his office and Ellie—ever Amanda's rival—wanted to know why.

"I can't tell you that, Ellie," George Brigham, Pinkerton's executive assistant, said.

"Why not, George?" Ellie asked.

"That's between Mr. Pinkerton and Amanda."

"George," Ellie said sweetly—a sure sign that the roof was about to fall in— "we both know that Amanda Foxworth*less* is not half the detective I am."

"That may be, Ellie," George said, "but you've got to admit she is gorgeous."

This infuriated Ellie Lennox and she exploded. "Is that all

you men can think of, how a woman looks? My God, George! I would have expected better from you."

"Ellie, I'm sorry—"

"And what am I, anyway? Dead wood?"

Ellie Lennox was definitely not dead wood, and George Brigham would be the first to admit that.

Ellie had long dark hair—the color of a starless night sky, to be precise. She was about five feet four with big brown eyes, a wide mouth, and full, firm breasts. She was pretty and never claimed to be anything else.

Amanda Foxworth, on the other hand, was about five feet ten with long, auburn hair, extremely long legs—or so it seemed, small yet firm breasts, and a classically beautiful face. She was able to move in circles that Ellie was not. When the job called for a woman to attend high society affairs, it went to Amanda. When it called for someone to masquerade as a tough-talking whore, it went to Ellie Lennox—and Ellie was sick of it.

"He's going to give her the McCloud case, isn't he?" she demanded of George Brigham. Pinkerton's assistant was a tall, slender man in his thirties who had no trouble whatsoever keeping the male Pinkerton agents in line. When it came to dealing with Ellie or Amanda, however, he was at something of a loss.

"Ellie—"

"Never mind, you don't have to tell me," she said angrily. "I know he is."

"Ellie—"

"I can solve this case, George," she said, waving that morning's *Denver Express* in his face. "You know I can, and you could have recommended me for it."

"Ellie—"

"And you would have if you weren't sleeping with that high-toned bitch!"

"Ellie!" he said, looking around his office to see if anyone else had heard. Satisfied that there was no one else in the room, he looked back at her and said, "That's a terrible thing to say."

"You deny that you're lying with that bitch?"

"No," he said, somewhat sheepishly, "but I am denying that it would affect my judgment."

"Ha! George, I've been here longer and I'm a better operative than she is. You know I deserve a shot at this case, not her."

"Your case will come along, Ellie," Brigham said. "I promise."

"Promises aren't good enough, Brigham!" she snapped. "Save those for your girl friend!"

She stormed out of Brigham's office and started down toward Pinkerton's. She had almost reached the door of the outer office when it opened and her rival, Amanda Foxworth, stepped out.

"There she is," Ellie said aloud, "old round heels Foxworth."

Amanda smiled her superior smile and, placing her hands on her hips, said, "What are you raging about?"

"You know," Ellie said. "Some women don't care how they get to the top, even if they have to sleep their way there."

Amanda raised her chin, looked down her nose, and said, "I guess you must have heard that the old man assigned me to the McCloud case. That's the only reason I can think of for this undignified attack—not that you've never been dignified."

"Undignify this," Ellie said, balling her fist and preparing to swing it. A hand caught her from behind, closing around her wrist, and she turned to look into the eyes of George Brigham.

"This is not the way, Ellie," Brigham said, "and neither is breaking in on Mr. Pinkerton. All that would accomplish is to get you fired."

Ellie pulled her wrist free of his grasp, glared at the two of them, and then turned and stalked off down the hall in the opposite direction.

"Thank you, darling," Amanda said.

"Amanda," he said, moving close to her as if to kiss her.

"Not here, George," she said, putting her hands on his chest to push him away. Staring off down the hall in Ellie Lennox's wake, she said, "She's angrier than I've ever seen her. What will she do?"

"Nothing," George Brigham said. "She's a good operative. Are we seeing each other tonight?" The tone of his voice was hopeful, and when he stared at her, he took on the countenance of an eager puppy staring at its master.

"I'm sorry, darling, not tonight. I've got to get to work on this case."

"Whom did he assign you to work with?" Brigham asked.

"Ken Sapir."

"Sapir?" Brigham was angry. He had recommended Amanda work with Carl Jeffers.

"He's the best detective we have, darling—and the handsomest."

"Amanda—"

"Don't worry, darling," she said sweetly, sweeping past him, "nothing will happen."

Brigham knew different. Sapir had never worked with a female operative and *not* slept with her. He was notorious for that. The only reason the old man kept him on was because he had lost Talbot Roper the previous year, Roper being possibly the best Pinkerton ever—although Pinkerton would never admit that outside the confines of his office. Without Roper,

Pinkerton needed Sapir even more, and as harsh as he had been on Roper, he went easy on Sapir.

Brigham stared after Amanda Foxworth, feeling shame and unbridled lust. The shame was because Ellie Lennox was right. She was the better of the two and did deserve to be assigned to the McCloud case.

Brigham was not sleeping with Ellie, however—though not from want of trying—and he was sleeping with Amanda Foxworth. Not only that, he was obsessed with the woman, and he knew that he was in an unhealthy position.

All he could think of, however, was the position he and Amanda had been in the night before and he wondered when—and if—they ever would be again, now that she had her big case to solve and make a name for herself.

# THREE

In the dining room of the Denver House Hotel, Clint Adams started his second pot of coffee and, once again, reached for his copy of the *Denver Express*. However, instead of returning to the news article, his curiosity prevailed and he turned instead to the center page and began to read.

As Amanda Foxworth walked away from George Brigham, her mind was racing. Sleeping with George had finally paid off, but now she filed him away as old news. The McCloud case would allow her to make her mark as a detective and impress Pinkerton. Of course, she'd have to put up with the egotistical Kenneth Sapir—and probably sleep with him—but he might end up being a help to her. He was a good detective, and if one of them solved the murder, they would both get the credit.

Of course, if *she* solved it, she'd do her best to cut Sapir right out.

She was worried about Ellie Lennox, though. As much as she hated to admit it, Ellie was a good detective, probably better than herself. But she had something to work with that Ellie didn't, and that was her fantastic beauty. It was a weapon she had used many times in the past, and it had served her well. The shorter, more buxom Ellie could not compete with that, she was sure.

Still, she'd have to watch out for her. If Pinkerton had assigned the case to Ellie instead of to her, she would have started working it on her own—and she was sure that Ellie Lennox was going to do the same.

Ellie Lennox hit the streets of Denver in a burning rage. She knew that she probably could have gotten the break she deserved long ago if she'd agreed to sleep with George Brigham when he first asked her to, but the truth of the matter was that the man disgusted her. He was manipulative and—in the hands of Amanda Foxworth—easy to manipulate, himself. She was glad he was sleeping with the bitch for one reason—when Pinkerton found out about it, George Brigham would be out on his ass.

She'd have to wait for that to happen, though, because she just wasn't the type to tell the old man herself. In fact, she was starting to think that she was too decent. It was time she stopped letting the George Brighams and the Amanda Foxworths of this world and, yes, even the Pinkertons, walk all over her.

She stopped on a street corner and unfolded the newspaper in her hands so she could read the headline again.

GRUESOME MURDER OF POLITICIAN'S WIFE IN HOTEL
ROOM!

Evelyn McCloud had been the picture of a devoted wife, and everyone said that when Alvin McCloud made it all the way to the White House she would make an excellent first lady.

Now she was dead and that wouldn't help his campaign at all. The newspapers would be watching him very carefully until the sensationalism of the case wore off, and by that time his political career might well be dead.

What about poor Mr. Chandler? she wondered. Dorothy Chandler's husband had been totally overshadowed by his willful wife, who was fighting tooth and nail for suffrage in Denver and all over the country. What about the fact that he had been murdered, too?

Ellie knew the way Amanda Foxworth's mind worked, and she knew that her rival would start her investigation at the top, with Congressman McCloud, the tall, handsome political figure and Denver society fixture. It would never occur to her that the intended victim might have been the other man, the one who had never appeared at a society function in his life.

Ellie decided to start her investigation—her unofficial investigation—from the other end, from the bottom.

She was going to talk to Dorothy Chandler and find out who might have wanted to kill her husband.

By the time Clint Adams reached the bottom of his second pot of coffee, he had finished the Hickok story. He told himself that he decided to read it simply to see if he was mentioned, but the truth was that he was curious about what it would say. To be sure, Hickok's talents and accomplishments had been exaggerated, but not by much. Similarly, the literary descriptions of his own accomplishments by J.T. Archer had been fairly accurate, though somewhat elaborate.

Clint had never liked dime novels or the people who wrote them, but perhaps he had been overly harsh in condemning them as a whole, as his waiter obviously did. Not wanting to be placed in the same category as the waiter, he decided that maybe he'd read a few more of these things before passing final judgment.

He refolded the paper, bringing him to the front page

again, and remembered the sensational murder story he'd begun reading over his first pot of coffee. He picked up the second coffee pot, found it empty, and decided to wait for another time to finish his reading. He did not want to keep the table from someone who had not yet eaten.

He rose, left a generous tip, as always, and left the dining room with the newspaper tucked beneath his arm.

Clint found himself a cushioned seat in the spacious Denver House lobby and finally settled down to finish reading the story of the murder. As he reread the opening paragraphs, he became aware of conversations going on around him, catching scraps here and there.

". . . terrible thing."

". . . disgrace to be in such a position."

". . . married to a wonderful man."

". . . no security . . ."

". . . shocking that it could happen *here,* of all places."

He looked up as he heard that last phrase and saw that the person who had spoken it, a well-dressed, middle-aged woman, was apparently leaving the hotel after having checked out. He frowned as he looked around and saw that there was a lot of activity taking place in the hotel lobby. Obviously, a lot of other people were checking out as well.

Could it be coincidence that this many people were checking out at one time?

Had something happened that he didn't know about? True, he had stayed late with Luisa and had a late breakfast, but wouldn't he have heard if something had happened, especially from his waiter?

For a second he was going to rise and ask the desk clerk what was going on when something struck him. He looked down at the newspaper in his lap and then picked it up to finish the story he'd started earlier in the day.

Several paragraphs down the name of the hotel where those ghastly murders had been committed appeared: the Denver House Hotel!

He folded the newspaper, stood up, and approached the desk.

"This looks like a mass exodus from a sinking ship," he commented to the tall, slick-haired young man standing behind the desk.

The man turned to him wearing an unconcerned expression that seemed a bit too contrived for his taste.

"Yes, sir, several people are leaving, but we have enough reservations to replace them. The Denver House will survive this crisis very nicely, thank you."

"Well, I'm glad to hear it," Clint said, "since I'm a guest here."

Apparently, the fact that he wasn't dressed like a Denver businessman had fooled the clerk who now looked as if he had committed a terrible error.

"Uh, sir, you're not checking out . . . are you?" he asked nervously.

"Me? After you just assured me of what a wonderful place this is? Of course not."

"I'm sorry, sir, if I seemed . . . preoccupied—"

"Don't mention it," Clint said, tapping the man on the shoulder with the newspaper. "This kind of thing can rattle anybody. Carry on."

"Uh, yes, sir. Thank you, sir."

Clint turned and surveyed the lobby. The clerk had been right. Although there were quite a few people leaving, the hotel was large enough so that they represented only a small portion of its clientele.

A question came to him as he was about to move away from the desk, and he turned to the clerk and said, "What room was that murder in?"

"Uh, sir," the man said, looking even more nervous, "I'm afraid that the staff is not permitted to discuss the, uh, incident." That might have explained why the waiter had not said anything.

"All I want to know is the room number," Clint repeated. "What harm can there be in that?"

"I'm afraid I can't—"

"Perhaps you'd better prepare my bill, after all."

Not wanting to be the cause of the hotel's losing another guest, the man looked about, swallowed, and said in a low voice, "Room three-fourteen."

"Damn," Clint said, turning away.

Could that be possible? he wondered. A murder of that magnitude had been committed in room 314 and he—who was in room 214—hadn't heard a thing!

Shaking his head, Clint mounted the steps that would take him to his room on the second floor. He did not see the dark-haired young woman who strode purposefully through the front door and up to the front desk.

# FOUR

Sometime later Clint Adams was still sitting in his room, pondering the fact that a murder—a double murder—had been committed in the room directly above his, while he had blissfully enjoyed the talents of Luisa Crowley. For much of the night, those unfortunate people could have been indulging in the same activity as he and Luisa, but at some point someone had entered the picture and changed all that.

Whoever the killer was he would have had to have spent a certain amount of time in the room to do what he had done, and how had he killed them so quietly?

He was in the midst of trying to make a decision—stay and take a chance on becoming involved in the murder or leave Denver the next morning—when someone knocked on his door. It was a strong, solid rap that led him to believe that the knocker would be a man.

He was wrong. He opened the door and was surprised to find a dark-haired young woman standing there.

"Can I help you?"

"You can if you're Clint Adams."

"I am."

"The Gunsmith?"

He winced and said, "Come inside, why don't you?"

The woman stepped past him and he closed the door and turned to face her.

"If you don't mind, I'd rather not hear that name right now." Or ever, he added to himself.

"You mean the Gunsmith?"

He winced again and said, "That's the one."

"I don't have time to ask you why, Mr. Adams," the woman said, "so I'll bow to your wish."

"Thank you. Am I supposed to know you?"

"Not at all," the woman said. She thrust her hand out at him like a man and said, "My name is Ellie Lennox."

"Ellie?"

"Well, it's actually Elena, but I don't use that in my business."

He knew he was going to regret asking, but he said, "Which is?"

"I'm a Pink."

"I'm sorry," Clint said, "you're a what?"

"A Pinkerton agent. A private detective."

"I see."

"And I need your help."

"With what?"

"This," the woman said, thrusting a newspaper at him. He recognized the *Denver Express,* saw that the paper was folded to reveal the murder headline, and then realized that debating whether to stay or leave had probably just cost him.

"I don't understand."

"I'm going to solve this murder, Mr. Adams, but I'll need your help to do it."

"Why me?"

"I need a man who is able to go into places I'm not."

"You don't understand," Clint said. "I mean why specifically me?"

"Because you're . . . who I said you were when you opened the door."

"Miss Lennox—"

"Since we're going to work together," she interrupted him, "you can call me Ellie."

"We are not going to work together, Miss Lennox—"

"That remains to be seen."

Clint took a deep breath and tried again. "Miss Lennox, how did you know I was staying in this hotel?"

"That's easy," she said. "I came across your name while I was checking through the registry downstairs."

"They let you see the registry?"

"The desk clerk did. I bribed him."

"I see."

"It's a useful, somewhat distasteful tool of the trade."

"I see," he said again.

"As soon as I saw your name there, I knew you were the man I needed."

"That's very flattering, but I'm not a detective."

"Don't be modest," she said, smiling knowingly. "We know all about what you did in that New York murder case earlier this year."

"That was a fluke."

"I think not, Mr. Adams, and I'm afraid you would not be able to convince me. You see, I've followed your career closely and I know that you have solved other crimes."

"Miss Lennox—"

"I know that you are not simply a gunman, as everyone who reads those dime novels seems to think. You were a lawman before you became known for your prowess with your gun, and you were a good one. You can do much more than shoot a pistol, Mr. Adams, and that's why I need you."

He gaped at her. The damn woman certainly had a way with words.

"What do you say?" she asked, sensing that she might have his interest piqued. "We can solve this one, you and I."

"Don't you have some detectives in your organization who would be better equipped to help you?"

"One man would," she said. "Ken Sapir."

"I've never heard of him."

"Have you heard of Talbot Roper?"

Clint had indeed heard of Roper. In fact, he'd met the man once or twice.

"He used to be a Pinkerton before he went out on his own."

"Exactly. Ken Sapir replaced him. He is not the best detective that Pinkerton has—or he is until I take that title."

"So, why not work with Sapir?"

"He has been assigned to work with one Amanda Foxworth." The distaste for the Foxworth woman was plain in Ellie Lennox's tone and on her face.

"And she is?"

"Another Pinkerton."

"Is she any good?"

"She is not technically a good detective, but she makes up for it in other ways."

Clint didn't bother asking what ways she used. He had a fair idea just by the way Ellie Lennox had said it.

"And you want to solve this case before she does?"

"I deserved to be assigned to the case, but that bitch is sleeping with Pinkerton's assistant, and he recommended her for the assignment."

"Tough break."

"Yes, indeed, but I intend to make the most of it . . . with your help. What is your answer, Mr. Adams."

"Call me Clint."

She smiled and said, "Then you agree?"

"No, Miss Lennox," he said, "I do not agree."

# FIVE

Amanda Foxworth entered the lobby of the Denver House Hotel just as Ellie Lennox was coming down the stairs. The tall blonde stepped behind a pillar and watched as Ellie stalked out of the hotel, obviously unhappy about something.

That made Amanda smile. She had gone to see Senator McCloud, but had been unable to get in to see him. She had bowed to the fact that the senator had arrangements to make and had accepted an appointment to see him the next day.

That left her free for the afternoon and she had cut herself loose from the clutches of Ken Sapir to do some checking at the hotel.

When she bribed the desk clerk to let her see the registry, she was totally unaware that she was the second person to have done so. The desk clerk had accepted her money and had the good sense to keep his mouth shut.

When she spotted the name of the man in room 214, she recognized it immediately and got an idea.

She was unaware that she was the second person to form that same idea in the space of forty minutes.

This time when the knock came at Clint Adams' door it was obviously a female's knock, gentle yet insistent.

25

He opened the door to find himself facing a tall, slender, well-built blonde of uncommon beauty.

"Mr. Adams?"

"That's right."

"You don't know me, but I have a proposition for you."

"Is that a fact?"

"May I come in?"

"Of course," he said, stepping back to allow the woman he felt sure was Amanda Foxworth to enter his room.

Amanda was quite different from Ellie in all respects but one—she, too, insisted that he call her by her first name. Beyond that the women were about as alike as his horse Duke and a pack mule.

Her story was the same as Ellie Lennox's, but she left out the part about partnering with Ken Sapir, reputedly Pinkerton's best operative.

Clint called her on it.

"Don't you already have a partner?"

"Yes, and he's quite good."

"But?"

"But he's not a living legend."

Clint hated being called that almost as much as he hated being called the Gunsmith. It made him feel so ancient.

"Miss Foxworth—"

"Amanda," she said, giving him a dazzling smile, "remember?"

"Yes, I remember," he said. "Miss Foxworth, I'm afraid I'm not available."

"Had another offer, did you?" she asked. "From Ellie Lennox?"

"As a matter of fact, yes. Miss Lennox was here."

"And what did you tell her?"

"I told her the same thing I'm telling you," he replied.

"The answer is no."

"She wouldn't accept that."

"You're right; she didn't. She said she'd call on me again tomorrow morning for my final decision."

"Well, then, I guess it's only fair you offer me the same chance."

"Fine," he said, "come by anytime. Come by together, why don't you?"

"I hardly think that's likely," she said. "We never do anything together."

"Then come by in the afternoon."

"What about tonight?"

"Tonight."

"Yes, for dinner. Are you free?"

Clint looked her up and down and liked what he saw. True, she was of a type, like Luisa Crowley, but she made Luisa Crowley look like a hag.

"For dinner."

"Yes, of course, for dinner," Amanda Foxworth said. "What else would I mean?"

Amanda Foxworth came back that evening for dinner. She was dressed, ready for an evening on the town, in a pink gown cut low over her small, firm breasts so that he could see plenty of cleavage. For a gal with breasts that were not overly large, she had some of the nicest cleavage he'd ever seen.

She took him to a small restaurant on Columbus Street that apparently catered to a society crowd. Everyone there was dressed as well as she, and Clint felt out of place in his black broadcloth suit.

"So what made you want to become a detective?" he asked her.

"What made you want to become a lawman?"

"Uh-uh," he said. "We're not here to talk about me or my past."

"Save that for when we're partners, huh?"

"We're not going to be partners, Amanda."

"No, don't give me your answer yet," she said. "The night is young and I may still convince you."

"Answer my question, then."

"My father was a detective—well, he was a policeman for a lot of years and then, after he retired, he became a detective." She got a faraway look in her eyes when she talked about her father. "I always thought he was the smartest, most wonderful man in the world, and when he died, I decided that I would become a detective, too."

"Do you have a knack for it?"

"Knack? No, not at all. I don't even really like it, to tell you the truth, but it's something that I have to do."

"Have you had much success?"

"I have, and do you know why?" She didn't give him a chance to answer. "It's because I'll do anything to get the job done."

"Anything?" he asked.

"Anything."


It was inevitable that they would end up in bed together. He knew that from the moment she walked into his room.

When they entered the second time, she turned to face him and said, "Do you have your answer ready yet?"

"Yes, Amanda. I can't—"

"Wait," she said, putting her fingers to his lips. "I haven't finished trying to convince you."

She pulled his head down to hers—and since she was tall it was not a chore—and kissed him, her tongue darting avidly into his mouth. There was no mistaking her intentions; she meant to go much further than just a kiss.

She pressed her body up against his; her hands probed between them, finding him and kneading him through his pants.

"If we're going to do this," he said huskily, "let's do it right."

He stepped back from her and began to unbuckle his gunbelt and then his belt. She smiled and started to undress. They watched each other, both liking what they saw when all of the clothing had been done away with.

They sank to his bed together, lips and hands busy, and eventually they ended up with her head between his legs.

She took his stalk in both of her hands and rolled it gently, flicking her tongue out from time to time to tease the swollen tip. Sliding one hand down the length of him, she took his balls in one hand and closed her other hand around the base of his erection. She slid her head forward and began to lick the length of him up and down until she stopped at the head and slid it into her mouth. Using her mouth and a hand—both equally talented—she began to bring him to the brink, only to stop him as he was about to come. He moaned and tensed as she took him into her mouth again, and he reached for her head to keep her from getting away. This time when she brought him to the brink she allowed him to flow over it, shooting into her mouth.

And that was just the beginning.

Later, while they were both getting dressed she smiled at him and said, "Now, I've given you my best argument. What's your answer?"

Feeling weak in the knees, he said, "My answer, Amanda, is no."

"What?" she asked, looking as if she'd just been slapped.

"No," he said again.

"But I—I just gave you the best sex you ever had in your life!" she said, incredulous at his answer. "And there's more where that came from."

"I'm sorry, Amanda," he said, "but this just isn't the way to buy me."

"Why, you—" she said, swinging her palm at him. He caught it before it could connect with his cheek and grabbed her by the wrist and held her that way.

"You did fine just now, Amanda, and with a lot of men it would have worked, but with me it was the wrong tack."

"But—but you let me!"

"You wanted to," he said. "It would have been ungentlemanly of me not to have let you."

"Ungentle—you don't even know the meaning of the word! I suppose you're going to help that cold bitch, Ellie Lennox? Well, let me tell you something, Clint Adams, the two of you together won't be able to solve this murder before I do."

He released her wrist and said, "You put a lot of faith in your body, Amanda, for someone who's just been turned down."

She tried to hit him again and he caught her easily again.

"As I said before, Amanda, we are not going to be partners, so perhaps it's time you leave. That is, unless you want to be bed partners for the night. I happen to have the night open."

She looked as if she wanted to slap him again, but thought better of it. Instead she snapped, "You should be so lucky, Clint Adams," and stormed out of the room, slamming the door behind her.

Weak-kneed still, he went to bed, sure that he had made the right decision, but wishing that she had decided to stay.

What kind of method, he wondered, would Ellie Lennox use the next morning?

# SIX

The following morning Clint was waiting in the lobby when Ellie Lennox arrived. He found that he was glad to see her, realizing then that he liked her. She looked fetching in a buckskin jacket, and that gave him another reason to like her. The way she dressed didn't make him feel shabby.

"Let's have breakfast," he said to her.

"I came here for my answer, Mr. Adams," she said. "I have work to do."

"I'll buy," he said, taking her by the elbow, and this time she didn't object. He steered her to the hotel dining room where they got a table and placed their order. He ordered his usual breakfast, while she simply ordered an egg, a biscuit, and coffee.

"Well, what's your answer?"

"A friend of yours came to my room right after you left yesterday."

"A friend of mine?" she asked. "Who?"

"Amanda Foxworth."

"She's no friend of mine!" she snapped. "What did she want?"

"The same thing you want."

"But she has Sapir."

"I know. I asked her if she had a partner."

"What did she say?"

He left out the part about his being a living legend and simply said, "She wanted me."

"Did you ask her why?"

"I think I know why," he said. He'd figured it out during the night. "I think she figures that she wouldn't have to share the credit with me, and she might have to with Sapir—if she finds the murderer."

"Oh, she'll try to get the credit. She'll probably sleep with him to get him to let her have the—wait a minute!" she said, suddenly looking suspicious. "What did you tell her?"

"I told her no, but she suggested that we have dinner and discuss it."

"Dinner?"

"That's right."

"Last night?"

"Yes."

Her face assumed a knowing look as she said, "And then I'll bet you both went to your room."

"Right again."

She made a face and said, "Damn you, you slept with her!" Several eyes turned their way, but she continued undaunted. "You slept with that bitch and now you're going to help her instead of me!"

"Wrong on both counts."

"Don't lie to me, Clint Adams. I don't know why it is that men just have to let her—"

"If you calm down, I'll tell you what happened," he said, interrupting her gently.

The waiter came to serve the breakfast and Ellie Lennox used the time to calm herself. Clint poured them both some coffee before speaking again.

"We did go to my room, but I did not sleep with her."

Technically, it was the truth—as long as Ellie didn't ask questions about anything further than that. "When I told her that I wouldn't help her, she tried to slap me and left."

"Because you rejected her?"

"Yes."

"Good for you!" she said, clapping her hands together happily. "I wish I could have seen the look on her face. Well, then, let's decide where we're going to start this investigation."

"Hold on a minute," he said. "I didn't say I'd help you, either."

She frowned at him and said, "But I thought you just said—"

"I just said I didn't want to help Amanda Foxworth."

"And why not?"

"Because I don't like her or her tactics."

"And what about me?"

"I like you a lot better, Ellie, but I really don't want to get involved in this."

"Aren't you interested in who could have committed a murder in the room directly above yours without you hearing a thing?"

She was sharp, which was another reason he liked her.

"I admit I'm curious—"

"Work with me then, Clint, and we'll find out the answer together. I'll share the credit with you, I swear!"

"That's not what I'm interested in, Ellie. You can have the credit."

"Then you will?"

To stall for time, he buttered a biscuit and asked her, "Is there anything in today's paper about it?"

"There sure is," she said, producing her copy of the *Denver Express* and handing it to him. "It made the front page with a picture of the senator."

He took it from her and opened it so he could see the front page—and froze.

"What is it?"

He turned the paper around so she could see it and pointed to the picture of Senator McCloud.

"Is this really a picture of McCloud?"

"Yes, it is. Why?"

He folded the paper and put it down on an empty chair next to him.

"We'd better finish our breakfast," he said then. "We've got a lot of work to do."

"You mean—"

"I mean you have a partner, Ellie . . . if you still want one."

They parted company, Ellie saying that she had to find out if they could get in to see Dorothy Chandler that day. Clint said that he also wanted to see Alvin McCloud, so she said she'd try to arrange that, too.

"I'm glad you decided to team up with me, Clint," she said before she left, "but I really wish I knew what turned the trick."

"Your charm, Ellie," he said, "just your charm."

She made a face at him and left, hoping to return within the hour with good news.

Clint went back to his room with Ellie's copy of the *Denver Express* and sat in a chair with the paper in his lap so that he could see the picture of Senator Alvin McCloud—only he didn't know the man in the picture by that name. He knew him as Owen McClain, one of the finest con men ever to work the east or the west.

Clint hadn't heard anything about McClain in the past eight years, but he'd never forgotten him. The man was the most natural actor he'd ever come across, which made him an ideal con man.

And, it seemed, a perfect politician.

Clint knew McClain and McClain knew him. He wondered what the man's reaction would be when they were eventually introduced.

# SEVEN

"Tell me about Mrs. Chandler."

They were in a buggy being driven to the Chandler residence. Ellie had returned with news that they had a luncheon appointment with Dorothy Chandler.

"She's a barracuda," Ellie said. "I don't like her one bit."

"Is there a woman in this town you do like?"

"My mother, up to last year," Ellie said.

"What happened last year?"

"She died."

"I'm sorry," he said. "Tell me about Mrs. Chandler."

"She's got money, which is why she can afford to spend all her time fighting for suffrage."

"You don't approve of women's suffrage?"

She said, "I believe in my right to be what I want, a detective, and to be given a fair chance to do well at it. So far, that hasn't happened."

"And Mrs. Chandler? What does she believe in?"

"She wants women to have the vote. Can you imagine that ever happening?"

"I've never thought about it. Why do you say that Mrs. Chandler is a barracuda?"

39

"You'll see," Ellie warned him. "Right there in her house, with her husband fresh in the ground and me standing at your side, she'll try to get into your pants."

"Do you think that she knew about her husband and Mrs. McCloud?"

"Who knows?" Ellie said. "But if she did, I don't think it would have mattered. She's slept with half the married and single men of means in Denver, and she never cared who knew it. What was her husband supposed to do?"

"Then you don't think that she killed them or had them killed?"

Ellie shook her head.

"There's no motive there, Clint," she said with certainty, "no motive at all."

"I don't know," he said. "My experience with women—"

"Has that been extensive?" she asked.

"My experience tells me that a woman is jealous, even when she says she's not."

"Is that a general statement applying to all women, Mr. Adams?"

"Most of the women I've ever known."

"I see."

There were a few awkward moments of silence before Clint broke through them.

"What about McCloud? What do you know about him?"

"Only what I've researched. He showed up in Denver about seven or eight years ago and immediately got into the mainstream of society here. He started in politics as old Senator Abbot's assistant and worked his way up from there. They say in three years he has a good shot at the presidency—that is, he did until this."

"What's going to hurt him most?" Clint asked. "The fact

that he's involved in a murder, or that his wife was cheating on him?''

"Both. Do you know a man who would want a man for president who can't even control his wife?''

"And the murder?''

"Well, we don't know that he's involved—''

"Personally involved,'' Clint said. "I'm not saying he did it—not yet, anyway—but he is personally involved.''

"Well, of course. His wife was murdered.''

"And Mr. Chandler, what was his first name?''

"Leon, and as far as the papers are concerned, he never existed. It's McCloud who's drawing the attention.''

"What about a sympathetic vote?''

"What do you mean?''

"How do you think the voters would react to a man who dedicated his campaign to the memory of his murdered wife?''

She thought that over a moment and then said, "That's not bad, Clint. Maybe you should go into politics. Or better still, maybe you should become a Pinkerton.''

"Working with a Pinkerton is bad enough.''

"What have you got against Pinkertons?''

"I've never made friends with one.''

"Well,'' she said, arching one eyebrow, "there's always a first time.''

They were let off in front of a two-story brick house with a fence around the front.

"The Chandler house,'' Ellie said.

"This is where she conducts her battle for suffrage from?''

"This is her base.''

"Some base.''

They ascended the front steps and knocked on the door,

using a large, ornate brass knocker.

When the door opened, a man appeared. He was a short man with white hair who wore a dark suit.

"May I help you?"

"Yes," Ellie said, "my name is Ellie Lennox, and we have an appointment with Mrs. Chandler."

"Step this way, please."

They followed the man through a large entry hall to a corridor and then to what appeared to be a den.

"Wait here, please."

Left alone, both of them stared about them in unabashed admiration.

"Some room, huh?" Ellie asked.

"It's something, all right."

The furniture was all plush and expensive, the drapes red brocade, the tables antique, and against one wall was a large and apparently well-stocked bar.

When the door opened, a woman who was probably Dorothy Chandler glided in and headed right for the bar.

"Mrs. Chandler?" Ellie said.

The woman positioned herself behind the bar and asked, "What will you have?"

"Nothing for me, thank you," Ellie said. "Mrs. Chandler—"

"And you, Mr. . . . ."

"Adams, Clint Adams, Mrs. Chandler. I'll just have whatever you're having."

"I'm having some sherry."

"Fine."

The woman poured two glasses, and Clint watched her. She was a handsome woman in her late forties with graying hair that still held some black, and she had a trim waist and a full-breasted body that made him wonder whether or not she wore a corset.

"You people are the Pinkertons?"

"My name is Ellie Lennox, Mrs. Chandler, and I am with Pinkerton," Ellie said. "Mr. Adams is assisting me in this investigation."

"Is Pinkerton short-handed?"

"Mr. Adams has some special . . . skills that our men don't have, Mrs. Chandler."

"Yes," Dorothy Chandler said, looking Clint up and down as he accepted his glass of sherry, "I'm sure he does. Well, tell me, what investigation is this, Miss . . ." She had forgotten Ellie's name already.

"Lennox," Ellie said, and Clint thought she was controlling herself very nicely. "We're investigating the murder of your husband and Mrs. McCloud."

"Oh, that," Dorothy Chandler said, "I thought the police were handling that."

"They are," Ellie said, "but we've been commissioned to look into it, too."

"By whom?"

"I'm afraid only Mr. Pinkerton knows that."

"Well, I'll have to ask him," Mrs. Chandler said, "won't I?"

"I suppose so, ma'am."

"All right," Mrs. Chandler said, assuming a put-upon expression, "ask me your questions quickly, please. I have an appointment in an hour."

"The questions are simple and to the point, Mrs. Chandler. Do you know of anyone who might have wanted to kill your husband?"

"You mean aside from Senator McCloud?"

"The senator threatened your husband?" Ellie asked.

"I didn't say that," Dorothy Chandler said, looking annoyed. "I simply said that he had a motive—that is, if he had found out about about Leon and his darling wife."

"Did you know about the affair, Mrs. Chandler?" Clint asked.

"Of course."

"Do you think Mr. McCloud did?"

"You'll have to ask him that, won't you?" she replied. "And to answer your other question, no, I don't know anyone who might have wanted to kill Leon. He was harmless."

"I see," Clint said.

"When did you see your husband last, Mrs. Chandler?" Ellie asked.

"The night he was killed. He told me he had to go out."

"Did he say where?" Clint asked.

"He never said where, Mr. Adams, and frankly, I never asked." She made a show of checking the expensive clock on the wall and said, "I'm afraid I can't really grant you much more time."

"I understood we were invited for lunch," Clint said, meeting her eyes.

Dorothy Chandler smiled an amused smile, frowned, and said, "Who told you that?"

Clint looked at Ellie who blushed and said, "Perhaps I misunderstood."

"I'm sure you did," Mrs. Chandler said. "It is I who have a luncheon to attend, and I simply must get ready. Will there be anything else?"

"Not at the moment," Clint said, "but we'd like to think we can count on your help in this."

"Of course, of course," she said, moving toward the door. "Call on me anytime."

"Thank you," Ellie said.

At the door Dorothy Chandler turned back to Clint and asked, "By the way, how was the sherry?"

"It is a little weak," he said, looking down at the glass he hadn't touched since his first sip.

"Yes," Dorothy Chandler said, looking somewhat puzzled, "It is, isn't it? I'm going to have to change brands."

And then she was gone. The small man returned and said, "I will show you out," and they followed him back to the front door.

After he'd shown them out, the little man climbed the stairs to the second floor and told Mrs. Chandler, "They're gone, ma'am."

"Very good, Hirsch."

She dropped her clothes to the floor and stood there naked in front of her man servant, who didn't bat an eye. He had long ago come to realize that he meant no more to his mistress than a stick of furniture, but knew that should he be caught staring at her he'd be fired instantly.

At forty-eight, Dorothy Chandler was still a luscious eyeful. Her breasts were still firm and high, her hips wide without being too fleshy. The only thing she'd lost over the past thirty years—from her days as a young dance hall girl and prostitute—was that tiny waist that had served to make her bosom seem even larger. Her waist was an acceptable twenty-five inches now, which was fine for a big woman, but there was a time when she'd been able to boast a nineteen-inch waist. Those days were long gone.

Dressing, she said, "Have Gunther bring the carriage around and send a message to Seantor McCloud that we have to talk tomorrow."

"Yes, ma'am," Hirsh said. He turned and left the room.

Still partly naked, Dorothy Chandler took a moment to examine herself in the mirror and she liked what she saw. She could still compete with young women like that lady Pinkerton, Ellie Lennox. She wondered if Clint Adams was sleeping with his partner. Well, no matter. She'd known from the first that she wanted him, and that meant that she'd get him by whatever means necessary.

That is, if he didn't get in the way, first.

"There's a lady who knows how to hide her grief well," Clint said.

"She's cold."

"And she didn't try to get into my pants."

"Don't sound so disappointed," Ellie said. "Besides, she looked you over pretty good."

"I didn't notice."

"Ha!"

"And what was that about being invited to lunch?" Clint asked. "Wishful thinking?"

"I just misunderstood, that's all. It was an honest mistake."

They didn't discuss anything more until they were in a buggy heading back to Clint's hotel. They had an appointment at the McCloud house, but it wasn't until that evening.

"You asked a lot of questions in there," Ellie Lennox said suddenly.

"I thought that was what we were there for."

"But I'm the one who's official—"

"Don't give me that, Ellie. What's Mrs. Chandler going to think when the Pinkertons who are officially assigned to this case show up?"

"She'll probably describe us and tell them we were there first," Ellie said with great satisfaction. "That should sit well with Amanda Foxworth."

"And what will happen to you when Pinkerton learns that you're working on this on your own."

"I expect he will either applaud my initiative," she said, "or fire me."

"By the way, who did engage the Pinkertons?"

"I wasn't kidding about that," Ellie said. "Only the boss knows that."

"I'd like to find out."

"Maybe you should ask him?"

"Yes," Clint said, "maybe I should."

# EIGHT

Clint and Ellie had lunch at the hotel and then parted company, agreeing to meet at an appointed hour so that they could go to the McCloud house together.

Ellie left the lobby and Clint went to the front desk.

"I'd like to send a telegram, please," he told the desk clerk. It was not the same man he had spoken to the day before, but you had to look very closely to see that, for they were so much alike.

"Please, sir, just go around the corner to the cage and the man there will take care of you."

Not so much alike. This one was immediately polite, without regard to whether Clint was a guest or not.

"Thank you."

Clint rounded the corner and stepped up to the cage, which was empty at the moment. He decided to wait and, in the meantime, surveyed the lobby. He had noticed that morning—and again now—that there was no mass exodus from the hotel today. Apparently, yesterday's clerk had been right, the Denver House had survived the bad publicity.

"Can I help you?"

He turned back to see a wizened man peering at him from between the bars of the cage. The man's face was a mass of wrinkles and lines that crossed each other, making his face seem as if it were covered by x's. There was a small patch of hair in the center of a bald dome that gleamed in the light, as if he waxed it.

"Yes, I'd like to send a telegram."

"Are you a guest?"

"Yes."

"Will you pay cash or have it added to you bill when you check out?"

"I'll pay cash."

"Very well." The old man retrieved a pad and pencil from beneath his counter and moved with what appeared to be exaggerated sloth—but was not, for that was the speed at which he moved—and said, "Proceed."

Clint proceeded, dictating a short message to be sent to Rick Hartman in Labyrinth, Texas, requesting whatever information Rick—who was a veritable fount of information—had on Owen McClain.

"If I'm not around when the reply comes in," Clint said, paying the clerk at the same time, "have it put in my box, will you?"

"Of course, sir," the man said. Clint gave the man something extra and the clerk said to him, "Have a good day, sir."

"Thank you. You, too."

Clint debated his next move: go to his room and wait for Ellie to return or go to the hotel bar for a beer? He decided to do both. First, he'd have a beer, and then he'd go to his room.

The hotel bar was not quite as lavishly furnished as the hotel lobby, but it sure came close. Even the seats at the tables had cushions on them.

The bartender was similar to ones found in every saloon, though. This one was the portly type, wearing a dirty apron and holding a dirty rag that he used to mop the bar periodically.

"What can I get you?"

"A beer."

"Comin' up."

When the bartender brought the beer back, he said to Clint, "You been here a week or so, ain't ya?"

"That's right."

"I seen ya come in a few times. Ya like it here in Denver?"

"It's a nice place to visit."

"Hear about the murders?"

"Yes."

"Somethin', huh? Right here in the hotel. Can ya beat that?"

"No, I can't."

"Room three-fourteen. Boy, that one's gonna get a lot of requests for a while."

Aware of human nature, Clint had to agree with the bartender. The curious and the morbid would be checking into the hotel and requesting room 314 for quite some time.

"I guess you're right."

The bartender mopped a spot that Clint could not see and said, "Fancy place, huh?"

"Pretty fancy," Clint said. He was content to drink his beer and give the bartender short answers.

"Yeah, a lot fancier than any place else I ever worked, I tell you that, but ya'd think a hotel as fancy as this would fix their room numbers, wouldn't ya?"

"What do you mean?"

"The room numbers here, on all four floors, they're messed up."

"How do you mean?"

"Well, for instance, take room three-fourteen, the one we was just talking about."

"What about it?"

"You'd think it would be right below room four-fourteen, wouldn't ya?"

"Well, of course. Why, isn't it?"

"Some of the rooms are, ya know, but others are messed up, like I told ya. You'd think they'd fix it, wouldn't ya?"

"Mmm," Clint said, frowning. "What about room two-fourteen?"

"What about it?"

"Is it directly below three-fourteen?"

"I wouldn't know," the man said. "I only heard about three-fourteen and four-fourteen. Why you interested?" the man continued, but Clint paid for his beer, left it on the bar half-finished, and walked out of the saloon at a rapid pace, leaving the bartender puzzled.

Clint rushed out to the lobby and mounted the stairs that led to the second floor and then hurried up the flight that led from the second to the third.

The hall he found himself in was very much like the one on his own floor, so he simply walked down to where his room would have been if he had been on the second floor. He stopped in front of the door and stared at the numbers on it: 313.

He turned around and looked behind him and to the right. He spotted 316 and then to the left he saw 314, the murder room.

The room numbers on the third floor were the reverse of what they were on the second floor. Even was on the right and odd on the left instead of the other way around. Just out of curiosity he went to the fourth and final floor and found that the numbers ran identical to the second floor.

It was not something he could readily explain—possibly just someone's careless error—but it did clarify something. It told him how two people could have been brutally murdered in a room supposedly directly above his without his hearing a sound.

They'd been killed in a room one floor up and across the hall. He didn't know exactly what, if anything, this meant, but he wanted some time to think about it.

He went back to his room and sat in the comfortable armchair the hotel supplied. Part of the reason he had agreed to work with Ellie Lennox had been his curiosity about how the murders could have taken place without his hearing anything, but that had been based on the murder room's being located directly above his—which it was not. So, he no longer had that curiosity to contend with. All he had left now was his interest in Alvin McCloud, who he knew as Owen McClain.

Was that reason enough to stay and get involved in a murder investigation for which he was not prepared to conduct?

He picked up the newspaper he'd left in his room earlier and stared at the photo again. McClain had gotten older, combed his hair differently, and shaved off his mustache, but it was still the same man; of that he was sure.

Well, he could always see McCloud/McClain tonight, satisfy his curiosity, and be on his way the next day. It wouldn't be fair to Ellie Lennox, but then she was actually in a race with her rival, Amanda Foxworth, to see who could solve the case first, and Clint really didn't like either's motive. Somebody should be working on the case because of caring about finding the killers.

And he certainly didn't fit that description any better than the two female Pinkertons did.

Down in the lobby a man approached the telegraph cage. The old clerk looked up and saw a dark-haired, square-jawed man in his mid-thirties and immediately decided he didn't like this fella's eyes. They were cold and hard, brown like two lumps of mud.

"Can I help you?"

"The man who was just there, a Mr. Adams, sent a message," the man said. "I'd like to see it, please."

"I can't do that, mister," the old man said. "That man's a guest at this hotel and as such he's entitled to his privacy."

"I see," the man said. He reached into his pocket and asked, "How much is privacy going for these days?"

"Five dollars?" the old man asked hopefully.

The younger man smiled and came out of his pocket holding a dollar.

"I'll give you a dollar, old man," he said, "and I won't reach between these bars and pull you out right through them. How's that?"

The old man fumbled about and finally handed the man the telegram Clint Adams had dictated. The man read it, nodded his head, and then gave it back with the dollar.

"Much obliged," he said and walked away, leaving the clerk sweating and shaking so much that the first two times he tried to send the message he made errors and had to start over again.

# NINE

Senator Alvin McCloud's house made Dorothy Chandler's look like a log cabin.

"A senator can afford this?" Clint asked as they approached the house. It was largely a brick affair with white pillars out front and a trellis beneath each window—which made for a lot of trellises.

"Not a senator's money," Ellie said, "family money."

"Her?"

"Right."

"What happens now that she's dead. Does the well run dry?"

"I'm afraid not," Ellie said. "A lot of people are committed to trying to get McCloud into the White House—"

"And they aren't going to let a little thing like a double murder stop them?"

"Not if they can help it."

Clint shook his head, glad that he had never gotten involved in politics beyond running for sheriff.

They knocked on the door and, as at the Chandler house, the door was opened by a servant, this one a black maid wearing a frilly white apron over a dark dress.

"Yes?"

"Ellie Lennox and Clint Adams to see Senator McCloud, please," Ellie said, and Clint winced.

When the maid went off to announce them and see if she should let them in, Clint leaned over and said in a low voice, "You gave them my name, too?"

"Why not?" she asked. "Is there anything wrong with that?"

Should he have told her that he knew that Alvin McCloud was not what he pretended to be and now that the man knew he was coming he would probably find some excuse not to see them? Better to wait and see what happened.

"No, nothing wrong," he said, shaking his head. "Nothing at all."

She gave him a puzzled look, but before she could ask a question, the maid returned with a man.

The man was tall and slender and dressed in a brown suit that cost more than any wardrobe Clint had ever had. He had brown hair that came to a widow's peak and a carefully trimmed mustache.

"Miss Lennox? Mr. Adams?"

"That's right," Ellie said.

"I'm Vincent Thurston, the senator's campaign and business manager."

He shook hands with both of them. He had a nice, strong, sincere handshake.

"Come this way, please. The senator is eager to talk to you both."

"Thank you," Ellie said, and they followed the man up a flight of stairs to the second floor.

"The senator has his office on the second floor to try to discourage anyone from breaking in."

"Seems to me the trellis under the window would be an open invitation."

Thurston looked at Clint and said, "Oh, you can't see the

senator's window from the front of the house. We've removed the trellis.''

''Good thinking.''

''Thank you,'' the man said, making it obvious that it had
been his idea.

''Here's his office,'' he said as they approached a closed
door. Thurston knocked and then opened it without waiting
for an answer.

''Alvin, the Pinkertons are here.''

''Fine,'' Alvin McCloud said.

The man had put on weight since Clint had seen him last,
but it became him. He was full in the chest and shoulders and
well-fed in the middle, but they combined to make him look
prosperous and competent. His hair needed cutting, but Clint
suspected that he wore it that way on purpose, so that he'd
look like one of the people. It was something Owen McClain
would have done to make him seem more sincere during a
con, so why shouldn't Seantor Alvin McCloud use the same
device during the big con?

''Miss Lennox?'' McCloud said.

''Yes,'' she said, approaching his desk. They shook hands
and she said, ''It's a pleasure to meet you.''

''And you.'' He looked past her at Clint and the Gunsmith
thought he could detect a bit of humor in the man's face as he
said, ''And Mr. Adams?''

''Yes.''

Clint shook hands with the man and found McCloud's grip
as tight and sincere as his manager's.

''Please, sit down, both of you,'' he invited. ''Vincent,
get us all some brandy, won't you?''

''Of course, Alvin.''

''Now,'' McCloud said, seating himself behind his desk,
''what can I do for you?''

Clint allowed Ellie to reply, content to sit back and watch a master con man at work on her.

"Well, we're investigating the tragic death of your wife and Mr. Chandler at the Denver House Hotel."

"Really? That's very interesting. On whose behalf are you doing this?"

"Well, the Pinkertons have been retained," Ellie said, "but only Mr. Pinkerton himself knows by whom."

"Mr. Pinkerton . . . and myself," the senator corrected her.

"Then it was you who hired us?"

"Yes," McCloud said, "as soon as I heard about the murder—but something puzzles me here."

"And what's that?"

"Well, I met the detectives assigned to the case earlier today. A Mr. Sapir and a lovely young lady named Amanda . . . Foxworth, I believe it was."

"Yes," Ellie said with distaste, "it is."

"So that leaves me puzzled about you two. When you arranged for this meeting, Miss Lennox, I agreed and then immediately checked you out."

"You did?"

"You are a Pinkerton, as you claimed, but your boss tells me that you are not assigned to the case."

"That's correct," Ellie said, deciding to bluff it out, "I'm working on my own time."

"And you, Mr. Adams," the senator said, ignoring Ellie for the time being, "you are not a Pinkerton, although I am told they tried on numerous occasions to hire you."

"That's true."

"It is?" Ellie asked, staring at Clint.

"Well, I know your reputation, Mr. Adams," the senator said, "and as for you, Miss Lennox, I've persuaded your boss not to fire you."

"You did?"

"I did."

At that point both Ellie and Clint accepted a glass of brandy from Vincent Thurston.

"Why?" Ellie asked.

"Because I feel the more people working on this case the better, and that includes the police, of course."

"Of course," Clint said.

"So I would like the two of you to continue your investigation."

"Will Miss Lennox be on salary while she does this?" Clint asked.

McCloud smiled and said, "I've arranged for that, too. In fact, Mr. Adams, I am in a position to offer you some recompense for your time."

"Is that a fact? And how much did you have in mind?"

"That remains to be seen—after the fact, Mr. Adams."

"We'll have to ask you some questions," Ellie said.

"Ask away."

"I have one," Clint said before Ellie could open her mouth. "You don't seem very upset over the death of your wife. Why is that?"

"Now, wait a minute!" Thurston said, taking a step toward Clint.

"Easy, Vincent," McCloud said. "These people are working for us now; they deserve an answer." He looked at Clint and said, "Let's just say that I am more concerned about the possible death of my campaign than I am about the death of my wife."

"Then why hire the Pinkertons? And us?"

"Because it is what I would be expected to do. I can't just sit back and allow the animals who killed my wife to go free. She was, after all, my wife, even if it was in name only."

"Alvin—" Thurston said warningly.

"Vincent, if they're going to do a thorough job they need all of the facts."

"Did you know your wife was seeing Chandler?" Ellie asked.

"Yes, I did."

"You didn't mind?"

"The marriage was over before that. We were staying together for the sake of appearance."

"Then you're saying that you're not a suspect because you didn't care about the affair?" Clint asked.

"I'm just giving you the facts, Mr. Adams—or may I call you Clint, since you're working for me."

"That's the second time you've said that I'm working for you," Clint said. "I don't recall accepting your offer, but sure, go ahead, call me Clint."

"In any case, Clint, I'm simply giving you all of the facts. If, from them, you draw the conclusion that I am not a suspect, that's up to you."

"Do you know anyone who might have wanted to kill your wife?" Ellie asked.

"How about Dorothy Chandler? She was, after all, the jilted wife."

"We've spoken to Mrs. Chandler," Clint said. "She's not all that upset about the death of her husband."

"Oh, dear," McCloud said, "I'm afraid the two lovers were being discreet for the wrong reasons."

"Senator," Thurston said at that point, "you have another appointment."

True or not, it was the same tactic Dorothy Chandler had used to get rid of them. Clint decided to allow it to work this time as well.

He stood up and Ellie, looking annoyed, stood up with him.

"We don't want to take up too much of your valuable

time," Clint said. "Will you be available to us for further questioning?"

"Just get in touch with Vincent, and he'll arrange it."

"Very well," Ellie said, putting her hand out. "Thank you for your cooperation."

"My pleasure."

Clint didn't bother to offer to shake hands and moved toward the door with Ellie.

"Clint," the senator said.

"Yes?"

"You and I should get together in the near future. I have an offer you might be interested in."

"You call it."

"I'll send a carriage for you."

"I'll be waiting."

Clint had no doubt that the next meeting would be on a one-to-one basis, and he wondered if Vincent Thurston knew who Senator Alvin McCloud really was.

# TEN

Outside Ellie turned on him and demanded, "All right, what was that all about?"

"What was what all about?"

"You know. You were rude to that man, Clint. What did you mean by asking him why he doesn't care that his wife is dead. That is an insult!"

"No, it isn't," Clint said. "It is true. He admitted it."

"It is still a rude remark. My God, the man's a senator!"

Clint kept his mouth shurt.

"Let's find a carriage."

He started off and she trotted in order to keep up with him.

"Tell me what's going on," she said.

"Nothing."

"Nothing, my ass! Why do I get the feeling that you know something I don't? I thought we were supposed to be partners?"

"That was your idea, not mine."

"But you accepted. Partners are supposed to share information, Clint. You're not sharing."

"Ellie—"

"Why does he want to see you alone? What kind of offer does he have?"

"How am I supposed to know?"

"I don't know how," she said. "I just know that you do. Come on, tell me."

"Ellie, as soon as I know something that I think you should know, I'll tell you. I promise."

"Why doesn't that promise fill me with a lot of confidence?"

"Have I ever lied to you before?"

"I don't find that to be a valid argument."

Clint spotted a carriage and waved at it. "Are you coming back to my hotel?" he asked.

"What for? You don't have anything you want to tell me, do you?"

"Not tonight."

"Then, I'll go home," she said. "I have to prepare to face my boss tomorrow."

"I can go with you."

She was about to refuse when she remembered something else that had been said inside.

"What was that business about Pinkerton's offering you a job?"

"He has on numerous occasions, and I turned him down each time. Of course, the last time was a long time ago."

"I thought you said you weren't a detective?"

"That was part of my argument to Pinkerton."

"So why did he want you?"

"He didn't want me," Clint said, "not the real me, anyway."

"Oh," she said. "Oh, I see. He didn't want Clint Adams as much as he wanted the Gunsmith."

"Right," he said, taking her elbow and guiding her into the carriage. "Have a good night's rest, Ellie. Come by my hotel in the morning and we'll go and see Pinkerton together."

"All right," she said, "but I hope you have more to tell me tomorrow than you did tonight."

"We'll see," he said, waving to her.

Clint watched until her carriage was out of sight and then turned to look back at the house, debating whether he should go back in. He decided to wait and let McCloud pick the time and place for their talk. Since there was a possibility that he was going to blow the man's entire campaign, he figured it was the least he could do.

Alvin McCloud, who had not been Owen McClain for almost seven years now, moved into the rooms across from his office and watched from his window as Clint Adams put the Pinkerton lady into a carriage. When the Gunsmith turned to look at the house, McCloud took an involuntary step back, but relaxed when the man turned and walked away, apparently seeking a carriage for hire himself.

As troublesome as Evelyn's death was going to be—more trouble than she was when she was alive, the bitch—Alvin McCloud knew that Clint Adams' presence was potentially disastrous. Something would have to be done about him.

"Senator?" Vincent Thurston said from behind.

He turned to find Thurston standing in the doorway with the light from the hall coming in from behind him. The man was holding his coat for him.

"Why are you standing in the dark, Alvin?" Thurston asked. "Is anything wrong?"

"No, Vincent," McClain said, turning away from the window, "nothing's wrong."

"You're going to be late," Thurston said, holding out the coat.

Senator Alvin McCloud slid into the proffered coat and followed his manager down to the first floor. If Thurston had asked him at that moment what appointment they were keeping, he would have been hard pressed to remember. His mind was exclusively on Clint Adams and the havoc the Gunsmith, a man from his past, could wreak on his present world . . . if he wanted to. McCloud was unwilling to wait to find out whether Clint Adams did or not want to.

Something would definitely have to be done about him . . . very soon.

# ELEVEN

The following morning Ellie joined Clint after he'd already had breakfast. He had waited for her to show up for some time before ordering.

"I ate without you," he said as she seated herself at his table in the hotel dining room.

"That's all right," she said. "I can't start eating breakfast with you every day, not the way you eat. I'd be fat in no time."

"You're not fat."

"Not now," she said. "I was once and I could be again if I'm not careful."

"When were you fat?"

"I don't think I want to discuss that with you here and now."

"Why not?"

"Because it has nothing to do with our partnership."

"Well, what if I told you it was a new condition of our partnership?"

"What? If I don't tell you about it, you'll quit?"

"Something like that."

She gaped at him and then said, "But that's blackmail—and it's silly!"

"You may be right," he said, standing up and enjoying her discomfort at thinking she may have to discuss something she was obviously unwilling to. "Why don't we get going? We don't want to keep Pinkerton waiting."

The office of the Pinkerton Detective Agency was in the center of Denver's busiest district. It was on the second floor of a prominent building—in fact, it was the second floor. As they approached the front door of the agency, Clint thought that the big eye painted on it might be staring at him somewhat balefully, as if asking him what the hell he was doing there. It was a question he was unwilling to answer at the time.

"Connie," Ellie said after they'd entered, "is Mr. Pinkerton in?" Connie was a severe, middle-aged woman sitting at the front desk, acting as receptionist.

"Mr. Pinkerton is always in. I'll tell Mr. Brigham you're here."

"I don't want to see George," Ellie said. "I want to see Mr. Pinkerton. That is, I believe he wants to see me."

"Be that as it may, you will just have to see Mr. Brigham first."

"Oh, all right, Connie."

As the woman rose and disappeared down a hallway, Clint said, "Don't tell me; let me guess. You don't like her, either."

"That's all right, though," Ellie said. "It's nothing personal, you see, because she doesn't like anyone—except Mr. Pinkerton himself."

Having met Pinkerton, Clint commented, "That's hard to believe."

They waited several minutes until the woman finally appeared with a man Clint disliked on sight. George Brigham had a self-centered attitude that showed on his face. It was an attribute—if indeed it could be called that—Clint had never liked in anyone.

"Ellie," Brigham said, pointedly ignoring Clint Adams, "the old man is not very happy with you."

"That just makes us even, George," she said. "Can we see him?"

The man looked at Clint now and asked, "This is Clint Adams?"

"That's right," Clint said, answering for himself.

Brigham looked Clint over briefly, then looked at Ellie, and said, "If the senator hadn't taken your side in this, Ellie, I don't know what would have happened."

"Sure you do, George," she said. "Can we see him now, please? We're keeping him waiting."

Brigham looked at Clint again, frowned, and then said, "Come this way."

"It's about time," Ellie said.

They followed Brigham down a hall to a closed door made of stout oak. He knocked. When there was a reply from inside—a totally unintelligible one, as far as Clint was concerned—Brigham opened the door and entered.

"Miss Lennox is here, sir," he said, and then as an afterthought he added, "and Mr. Adams."

Pinkerton rose from behind his desk. He was a portly, white-haired man with chubby hands.

"All right, George," Pinkerton said. "Thank you. You can leave now."

"Sir, perhaps I should stay—"

"Perhaps you shouldn't, George," Pinkerton said, giving the younger man a long, pointed stare.

"Yes, sir," Brigham said unhappily. He backed out of the room and closed the door behind him.

Clint expected Pinkerton to seat himself then, but he remained standing and looked at Ellie Lennox.

"You have initiative, young lady."

"Thank—"

"That might be an admirable trait in some people, but not in people who work for me."

"I hope that's not true, sir."

"Why?"

"If it is, I don't think I'd want to work for you anymore."

Pinkerton stared at her for a few moments and then said, "You've got spunk, too."

"Is that another admirable trait?" Clint asked.

"I'll get to you in a moment, Adams," Pinkerton said, not taking his eyes off Ellie. "What do you have to say for yourself, young woman?"

"You made a mistake, Mr. Pinkerton, when you assigned Amanda Foxworth to the Denver House murders."

"And you were trying to save me from myself? Is that the way of it?"

"I wouldn't exactly put it that way, sir."

"Mr. Brigham thought that Miss Foxworth was exactly the right person for this case," Pinkerton said. "What makes you think she isn't?"

There it was, the perfect opening. She could have taken advantage of it and blurted out that George Brigham was sleeping with Amanda, but instead she allowed it to pass.

Pinkerton, however, did not. "Of course," he said before she could reply, "he is having it off with her, isn't he?"

"Sir?" she said, puzzled. He knows about that? she wondered.

"Of course, I realize that," he said, as if reading her mind. "I make it my business to know everything about my people."

"But sir—"

"But what?" he asked. "Why haven't I fired him? That's quite simple. I haven't found a replacement for him yet.

When I do, he will be gone." He winked at Ellie then—a move that shocked her—and said, "But that will be just between us for now, eh?"

"Of course, sir."

"You didn't answer my question, Miss Lennox," he said then. "Why would you be better qualified for this case than Miss Foxworth?"

"I'm a better detective than she is, sir."

"That was never in doubt, Miss Lennox, never in doubt," he said, shocking Ellie further and pleasing her. "She does, however, possess certain talents that she might put to good use in this case."

"If that's the way you feel, sir."

"That is the way I feel, but that doesn't make a difference to you, does it? You'll go on working on the case anyway, won't you?"

"Yes, sir."

"Assisted by Mr. Adams, I assume."

"We're working together, sir," Ellie said, dispelling the notion that either one was simply assisting the other. Clint was impressed with her for that, and so apparently was Pinkerton.

"Senator McCloud has asked that you be left on this case, Miss Lennox, working from a direction different from that of Miss Foxworth and Mr. Sapir."

"Yes, sir."

"There's a condition you must understand, however."

"Which is, sir?"

"Your job depends on this case," Pinkerton said. "I want you to understand this well, Miss Lennox. If you do not solve this case, I will fire you."

"And if I do?"

"Then your talents will be put to much better use than they have been thus far during your employment."

Ellie hesitated a moment and then said, "Agreed."

"I was not putting that up to be agreed to or disagreed on by you. I was stating a fact."

Ellie didn't know what to say to that, so she kept silent.

"Having heard everything I've said," Pinkerton said, turning his attention to Clint Adams, "do you still intend to work with Miss Lennox?"

"I intend to help her in any way I can."

"Then I have one question for you, sir."

"What is it?"

"When this is over, will you come to work for me?"

"I've answered that question several times before, Mr. Pinkerton," Clint pointed out. "Nothing personal, but the answer is still the same."

"Bah!" Pinkerton said, finally seating himself again. "Get out, both of you, and do what you have to do. Keep me informed of your progress, Miss Lennox."

"Directly, sir?"

"Yes, damn it, directly."

"Yes, sir!"

They left the office, Clint grudgingly admitting to some respect for the irascible older man. He apparently knew that Ellie Lennox had some talent as a detective, and by putting her back against the wall he was expecting to draw the best out of her.

Clint couldn't wait to get started now.

# TWELVE

Amanda turned over in bed and looked down at the man she had spent the night with. He had meant little to her in the beginning, just another man she could use for her own purposes, but slowly she had found herself feeling something that she'd never felt with another man—both sexually and emotionally. It was disconcerting to say the least and at the same time it was a wonderful feeling. She'd never had such marvelous sex with a man before—unless you counted Clint Adams—but thoughts like that could lead to problems she wasn't ready to deal with.

However, she couldn't afford to allow it to interfere with her work.

"Pinkerton is seeing Ellie Lennox and Adams this morning," she said to him.

"So?"

"So maybe he's going to pull her off the case."

"A case she was never officially on?" her lover said disdainfully. "Come on, Amanda. Don't underestimate your opposition."

"Believe me, I don't underestimate Ellie."

"Just as I won't underestimate Clint Adams. The man's reputation—"

"No one could have a reputation like that and have it all be true," she said. "I thought he was just a legend, like Wild Bill Hickok."

"Sweetheart," the man said, speaking as someone both older and wiser, "Hickok was no Legend built on nothing, and neither is the Gunsmith. This man is deadly. He's probably the best there is right now, and the best there will ever be for a long time."

"With a gun, maybe," she said, "but what about as a detective?"

"He hasn't got too much of a rep in that area, but believe me, he's no amateur."

"Then what do we do? He should be getting a reply from that telegram you found out about. Maybe you shouldn't have let it go through."

"It won't help him with the case," the man assured her.

"I think he should be stopped."

The man turned his head and stared at her with his cold eyes which, only the night before, had smoldered with passion. Now, they caused a chill to pass through her.

"What do you mean stopped?"

"He shouldn't be allowed to interfere," she said. "He just might help Ellie solve this thing before I do."

"Are you saying you want him killed?"

"*Could* you kill him?"

"I can kill anyone."

"Would you?" she asked, rubbing herself against him. Only half serious, she asked, "Would you kill him . . . for me?"

"For you?" he asked. "Hell, no."

She stiffened and was about to pull away when his strong right arm encircled her and he said, "But for *us*, sure I would."

●     ●     ●

When Clint and Ellie returned to his hotel, the reply to his telegram was waiting in his box, along with another message. He accepted them both and read them.

"What do they say?"

He folded them up and asked, "Do I read your mail?"

She frowned angrily and said, "So help me, Clint, if you're keeping something from me—"

"Why would I keep something from you?" he asked. "Didn't I tell your boss that I was in this with you until the end?"

"That *was* nice of you."

"Sure, it was. I'm a real nice guy," he said, slipping both pieces of paper into his pocket.

"You are," she said, but he was glad to see she let the subject of his messages pass. "We've got to decide what our next move is."

"You worried about your job?"

"Hell, no," she said. "Even if I get fired, if I can solve this case my reputation will be made in this town."

"But if you solve it, you won't get fired."

"Maybe not," she said. "Maybe I'll quit."

"Whoa, girl, let's not go off half-cocked. Let's do this thing one step at a time."

"Right. What's our next step?"

"Well . . ." he said and told her.

Her eyes lit up and she said, "I like it. It's wicked and deceitful and—"

"Never mind what it is," he said, pressing his hand against the small of her back to get her moving, "let's just do it."

# THIRTEEN

Clint sat in his hotel room, waiting and wondering if his impromptu plan would work and, at the same time, doubting that it would. He had a feeling that Amanda Foxworth, and especially a man like Ken Sapir, would not be fooled so easily.

When a knock came on the door, he had just about convinced himself that it would be Ellie, announcing that her part of the plan had failed.

"Why are you so surprised?" Amanda Foxworth asked. "I got a message at the office that you wanted to see me. It was from you, wasn't it?"

"Oh, yes, it was," he said, backing away to allow her to enter. "Come in."

"What was it you wanted to see me about?"

"I wanted to apologize," Clint said, closing the door and turning to face her.

"For what?"

"For the way I treated you. It was uncalled for. You were right; I should have stopped things before they went too far, but I was . . ."

"You were . . . what?" she asked, frowning at him.

"Too attracted to you to let you get away," he finished.

This part he'd get away with, he was sure, because women like Amanda Foxworth were vain and believed in the power of their own beauty.

"Really?" she asked.

"Yes, really," he said, moving closer to her. "I haven't seen a woman as lovely as you, or as exciting in bed, in a long time."

"And what do you expect all this flattery to do?" she asked. "Turn my head? Get me back into bed with you? Or perhaps let you know how I'm progressing on the McCloud murder case."

"McCloud and Chandler," he reminded her, "but I don't want to talk about that."

"You don't?"

"No."

He took her by the shoulders and held her firmly.

"I haven't been able to get you out of my mind, Amanda."

"Clint, I don't know what to say."

"Don't say anything," he said. He drew her close so that his lips were less than an inch from hers. "I know I have a lot of nerve doing this, and you can push me away if you want."

He waited and when it was obvious that she was not going to push him away, he kissed her, a gentle touching of the lips. It was she who increased the pressure, sliding her arms around his neck and slipping her tongue into his mouth.

His hands played with the catches and buttons on her dress, and then it was down around her ankles. He removed her undergarments, kissing the flesh that he was exposing. He took her nipples in his mouth and suckled them until they were hard and then continued down over her belly until his face was nestled between her legs. She gasped as his tongue probed, and she took two steps back until the bed struck her behind the knees. She fell onto the bed and he took the opportunity to remove his own clothes.

He was naked when he joined her on the bed and her hands slid down to take hold of his rigid cock. He put his arms around her, holding her close, her flesh burning his. He kissed her neck, her cheeks, her chin, the other side of her neck, and the whole time she had a tight grip on him and was pumping him up and down.

"Let me," she said then, eagerly scrambling down between his legs. He felt her hot, wet mouth slide down over him, and took her head in his hands. He allowed her to move at her own tempo, her lips and teeth sliding up and down the length of him, and suddenly he felt a rush coming up from his legs into his loins and he exploded into her mouth . . .

They made love twice and then lay together among the tangled, damp sheets, pleasantly exhausted.

"That was wonderful," she said.

"Yes, it was," he said and meant it. She was inventive and without inhibition in bed, and now he felt almost guilty about the way he was using her—but damn it, it's the way she had wanted to use him!

"What happened between you and Ellie?" Amanda asked then.

"What do you mean?" he asked innocently. "Why should something have happened?"

"I understand that you are working with her."

"Oh, I am."

"Then why send for me?"

"I told you. I wanted to apologize."

"Well, you certainly have a marvelous way of doing that, but I don't believe you."

"What?" he asked, contriving to sound hurt.

"I don't believe that that's the only reason you wanted me to come here."

"Well," he said, "I do want to see this case solved, but to

tell you the truth, I don't much care who gets the credit.''

"Well, that's where we differ," she said, "because I do care. I want the credit."

"Well, you can have it."

"Wait a minute," she said, propping herself up on an elbow, causing the sheet to fall away and exposing her perfect right breast and its pink nipple. "Are you telling me that you want to exchange information? You want me to tell you what I know, and you'll tell me what you and Ellie know—"

"And when the case is solved, you can have the credit," he finished for her.

"That's an interesting proposition," she said. "What do you know?"

There was no harm in telling her the truth because they didn't know all that much.

"Not much. We talked to Seantor McCloud and Mrs. Chandler, and neither of them seems to be broken up about the murder."

"I noticed that, too—and the senator should be because this murder could break his campaign into little pieces."

"I agree," he said, "so there's something there that's not right. Did either of them give you any suspects?"

"No," she said. "Actually, I expected them to come up with some names, if just to throw themselves into a better light, but neither one did. It's as if they don't want to help."

"If that's the case, why did McCloud retain the Pinkertons?" Clint asked, wanting to see if she, too, knew the answer.

"His position demanded he do something, but that doesn't mean he has to be a big help, does it?"

"I guess not."

She snuggled up to him and said, "All right, so neither of

us knows much now, but later we each should be able to come up with something that will help.''

"I'm sure we will," Clint said, reaching for her breast with his tongue. "Meanwhile," he said with his mouth on her breast, "I've got something that will help right now!"

She closed her eyes, let her head loll back on her shoulders, leaned into him, and said, "Oh, yes!"

Ellie Lennox did not use quite the same tactics that Clint Adams did.

After leaving the message for Amanda at the front desk, without letting anyone see her do it, she had sought out Ken Sapir and inquired about his progress on the case.

"Is this idle curiosity?" he asked.

"Not really," she said. "I'm working on it as well."

"Really? Does the boss know about this?"

"Yes."

"Well, I don't know what to tell you, Ellie—"

"Just tell me what you've got so far, Ken."

"I don't think—"

"Come on. You're not worried about who gets the credit for this one, are you? The important thing is to find out who killed those two people."

"Oh, I agree with you, Ellie," Sapir said, "but I'll have to talk to my partner before we execute any kind of tradeoff of information." He peered at her closely and said, "That was what you were suggesting, wasn't it? A straight trade?"

"Of course."

"Well, let me talk to Amanda and I'll see you about it tomorrow, OK?"

"Sure," Ellie said, realizing suddenly that she and Clint had made a tactical error, "fine. See you tomorrow."

# FOURTEEN

Ellie Lennox arrived soon after Amanda Foxworth had left, and when she saw the rumpled sheets that Clint had not had a chance to straighten, she frowned.

"Did you have to do it that way?"

"It's the only language she understands, Ellie," Clint explained. "I had to act out the part of a man so enchanted by her beauty that I'd be willing to trade secrets with her . . . in bed."

"That's her style, all right," Ellie said, "but I didn't think it was yours."

What was she sore about, anyway?"

That same thought was in both of their heads at the same time.

"How about you and Sapir?"

"I didn't throw myself into his bed, if that's what you mean," she said a mite haughtily. "I appealed to him as a professional, told him that the important thing is to get this case solved and not worry about who gets the credit."

"What did he say to that?"

She scowled and said, "He said he'd have to talk to his partner about it."

"Do you think he will?"

"I hope not," Ellie said, "because it will look too much like a coincidence for both of us to want to exchange information."

"We should have thought of that before," Clint responded, admitting to himself—as Ellie Lennox had done earlier—that they may have made a tactical error.

"We'll just have to wait and see what happens," Ellie said. "Meanwhile, let's get that bed of yours stripped and changed."

Amanda Foxworth left Clint Adams' room in a state of confusion.

She wasn't confused about his wanting to exchange information and wanting her to have the credit for solving the case. Actually, she didn't quite believe him. No, what she was confused about was the way she had responded to him in bed on both occasions. She had two men in her life now who were drawing her out during sex as no man had done before.

That was confusing.

She was determined, however, to concentrate on the business at hand, and she was not at all keen on passing any information to Clint Adams—at least not until she was sure that he wouldn't just pass it right on to Ellie Lennox.

George Brigham frowned as Ken Sapir entered his office. Sapir was a good-looking, square-jawed man in his mid-thirties. Was the man sleeping with Amanda yet?

"What is it, Sapir?"

"I want to know about Ellie Lennox's status on this double murder, George."

"She has Mr. Pinkerton's personal go-ahead to work on it."

"Alone?"

"There is no other operative assigned to her."

"What about this Clint Adams?"

"Mr. Pinkerton didn't say," Brigham said, and he was obviously uncomfortable about admitting that. He was Pinkerton's assistant; he *should* have been told everything, and he hadn't been. Of that he was sure.

"All right," Sapir said, "thanks." He turned to head for the door and Brigham stopped him.

"Ken."

Sapir turned, surprised to hear the man use his first name. The best way to describe their relationship would have been strained. Sapir had absolutely no regard for Brigham as a Pinkerton or as a man, and Brigham reacted to Sapir's personality adversely—which was the way he reacted to any man who had a personality, since he did not.

"Yes?"

"How are you and Amanda Foxworth getting along on this case?"

"Fine," the man replied—smugly, Brigham thought.

In fact, Sapir knew what Brigham was leading up to, and it was his pleasure to keep the man guessing, even though he knew that nothing had happened—yet.

"No problems?"

"None at all," Sapir said, smiling broadly. "We get along just great."

"Yes, all right," Brigham said. "That's all." Bastard! he thought.

After Ellie Lennox left Clint's room, the Gunsmith sat down and took out the telegram and the message he had picked up at the front desk.

The telegram was from Rick Hartman who said that Owen McClain had been one of the best con men he'd ever seen, but had dropped out of sight about eight years ago without apparent cause or explanation. Rick also suggested that the reason for McClain's disappearance was generally considered to have something to do with a big con. To Clint, it looked as if Rick were right.

The message that had been waiting in his box was also very interesting. It was from Senator McCloud himself. It said that he would be sending his carriage for Clint that evening so that they could have dinner together and chat about old times.

Folding the two pieces of paper, Clint felt a twinge of guilt about holding out on Ellie, but he wanted to talk to McCloud before he did anything to give the man's real identity away—if indeed he would.

Now he was going to have his chance to talk.

# FIFTEEN

Clint was waiting in the lobby when his host's driver entered and looked around.

"Are you driving for the senator?" Clint asked.

The driver, tall and rangy and with piercing eyes, said, "I have that pleasure, sir. Are you Mr. Adams?"

"I am."

"The senator is waiting, sir."

"Well, by all means, let's not keep the senator waiting," Clint said.

"This way, sir."

The man's carriage was waiting right out front. Clint climbed in the back. The driver climbed up into his seat, took up the reins, and started off.

Clint had seen much of Denver. That was, after all, his reason for coming. He'd been impressed by the city, its brick structures, most of them businesses of one sort or another, its cobblestone and gravel streets in some sections, its huge and seemingly orderly population. In a way, Clint hoped that Denver's growth reflected the future of the entire west, although he realized that such growth would likely make men like himself virtually obsolete.

The drive was a short one and terminated in a small,

slanted street that seemed to be populated on both sides by small shops. The carriage stopped in front of a small restaurant and the driver stepped down.

"Here we are, sir."

"Where are we?" Clint asked, dropping down to the street himself.

"This is one of the senator's favorite restaurants, sir."

"It's a little out of the way, isn't it?"

"It has charm, sir."

"Yes," Clint said, and he added mentally, it's a great place for a secret meeting.

"He's waiting inside, sir."

"Thank you. Are you coming in?"

"No, sir. I shall be here when you're ready to return to your hotel."

"And how will the senator get back home?"

"He has made arrangements."

"I see."

The meeting seemed planned well, and Clint started to wonder if it couldn't also be described as a trap. He was, after all, a potential threat to Owen McClain's political future as Alvin McCloud.

"Thank you," he said again to the driver and stepped inside the small restaurant. He was not surprised to find that the quaint, rather close little establishment was empty save for one individual seated at a table in the center of the room, which had been cleared away for this purpose.

McCloud looked up at the sound of the opening door, smiled, and beckoned to Clint. There was a waiter standing against one wall, but he made no move toward the table and probably wouldn't until he was called.

"Good evening, Clint," McCloud said as Clint neared his table.

"What do I call you?" Clint asked, "Senator? Alvin? Or—"

"I'd appreciate either one," the man said, cutting him short, "and I'd also appreciate your keeping yourself confined to those two choices for the time being."

"Whatever you say," Clint said, seating himself. "You're buying—you *are* buying, aren't you?"

"Oh, definitely," the man said, waving to the waiter now. "Do you mind if I order for both of us? This is really an excellent restaurant."

"Go ahead," Clint said, "order. I've got other things on my mind."

"I thought you might."

He gave the waiter their order, heeding Clint's sole request for a pot of strong coffee.

When the waiter was gone, Clint asked, "So what have you been up to for the past eight years?"

"Just what you see," the man said, rubbing his fingers over the lapels of his expensive jacket.

"The big con."

"Oh, it might have started out that way," McCloud admitted, "but I was eventually bitten by the bug."

"Which bug is that?"

"The political bug."

"Well, I have to admit, you didn't step all that far out of your class."

"I agree," the senator said. "Politics is really just one big con."

"And your rise seems to have been—"

"Meteoric. That's the way one newspaper scribe put it."

"I don't put much store in what most newspapermen print in their papers."

"Oh, that's right. It was a newspaperman who christened you the Gunsmith."

"I'd appreciate it if we didn't make reference to that again."

"As you wish," the senator said. "After all, you are my guest."

"I'm a little puzzled about that. Why am I your guest?"

"Well, I appreciated the way you kept our secret during that meeting at my house. You still haven't let your partner in on it, have you?"

"No," Clint said, "not yet."

"Good. I hope to convince you that there's no necessity for it."

"You don't think that the voters have a right to know that they're being represented by a man with a false name and background?"

"That's the whole beauty of this setup, Clint," the man said, and with his eyes shining, he looked a lot like the old Owen McClain. "The name and background are not false. They're genuine."

"How's that?"

"A little over seven years ago I met the real Alvin McCloud. He wasn't much at the time. In fact, he didn't even want to go into politics the way his family wanted him to, and he was virtually on the run from it."

"Where was this?"

"Tucson."

"What happened to him?"

"He was killed—I had nothing to do with it. We got into a poker game and he called one of the players for cheating. The man took offense and drew on him. He shot McCloud and I shot him. I hauled McCloud off to a doctor, but it was no use. He was finished."

"So you helped yourself to his name and identity."

"He asked me to," McCloud said. "In fact, he begged me to. He said he knew he was dying and now he was sorry that

he had run from the future his family—his father, actually—
had planned for him. Clint, he cried like a baby and asked me
to take up his life for him.''

"And you couldn't resist a challenge like that.''

"Hell, no. What self-respecting con''—and he lowered
his voice here—''con man could have?''

"So you came here as Alvin McCloud?''

"He gave me his wallet, his identification, everything I
needed to become him.''

"How did his wife react to that?''

"She didn't come into the picture until after I came back.
That mistake was all mine.''

"And how long did you intend to go on with it?''

"Not long, really. I just wanted to see if I could get away
with it. See, Alvin was brought up in the east and his father
sent for him to come west to make his fortune.''

"So nobody in Denver knew what he looked like?''

"They had a vague notion, but the two of us were similar
enough physically for me to pass.''

"And what about his father?'' Clint asked. "Don't tell me
he didn't know you weren't his son.''

The waiter came with their food then and the conversation
was suspended until he had served and left.

"Boy, I want to tell you, that's the strangest part of all of
this. I had sent a telegram ahead letting his father know that
Alvin was coming. When I got to Denver, I went to his
father's house to explain things to him. When I got there, he
had some people there with him. He took one look at me,
Clint, and he knew damn well I wasn't his son, but he never
let on.''

"What are you talking about?''

"That old fox introduced me to everyone as his son Alvin!''

"That's crazy.''

"You know what's even crazier? When they all left that evening, he turned to me and he said, 'I don't want to hear about it. From this moment on, you are my son.' "

"What did you say?"

"What could I say? The whole crazy business was becoming harder and harder to resist. I said, 'Yes, father,' and we never discussed the matter again. You know, I think the old geezer was proud as hell of me right up until the day he died."

"When was that?"

"Two years ago," McCloud said, "a week after I was elected senator."

Clint almost asked McCloud how the old man died, but realized that that was something he could look up very easily.

"All right, no more talk. Dig into that steak and tell me it's not the best you ever ate."

"You don't want to discuss this further, Alvin?"

"What's to discuss?" the man said, picking up his own knife and fork. "You know the entire story now, Clint. The rest is up to you. I'll be watching the newspapers for the next few days. If nothing shows up, I'll assume that you decided to keep our secret."

"Does anyone else know?"

"One person."

"Your manager?"

"No, he came into it after the fact, the way my wife did."

"Senator," Clint said, "let's talk about your wife."

"Oh, that," he said, making a face. "You're going to ruin my meal with talk about that woman."

"Who killed her?"

"Damned if I know. If I did, I'd give him a medal."

"Don't you think that her murder and the circumstances surrounding it are going to damage your career?"

"Are you serious? Do you realize what a martyr I've

become in the eyes of my voters? I'm only sorry women don't have the vote. I tell you, they'd eat this up!''

''And you really have no idea who killed her?''

''None.''

''Or if she was the intended victim?''

''You're thinking that one of them was the victim and the other an innocent bystander?''

''It's possible.''

He frowned then, considering the question, and then said, ''I think I can rule her out as the intended victim.''

''Why is that?''

''She kept to herself, Clint. She never made any enemies, unless you count Dorothy Chandler.''

''Dorothy Chandler claims that she didn't care about their affair.''

''I'm sure she's being honest, but she still hated Evelyn's guts.''

''Why?''

''Jealousy, Clint. What other reason does a woman need to hate another woman? Evelyn was a beautiful woman and was fast becoming the belle of the Denver social circle.''

''A title previously held by Mrs. Chandler?''

''Yes.''

''How long were you and Evelyn married?''

''We got married just before the election two years ago,'' the man replied immediately without the usual hesitation that plagued most men when faced with that question.

Clint recognized the marriage as a possible ploy to get votes and asked, ''Whose idea was that?''

''Thurston's, and it was a grand one. I don't know how many votes I must have gotten as wedding presents, but they must have put me over the top. I never would have gotten that many votes as a bachelor—but I still might have won. Many are the times I wish I had tried.''

Staring at McCloud, Clint realized that the man was just as much in his element as he had ever been.

"I told you," the senator said, reading the look on Clint's face, "there's not much difference between this and what I was doing before—and I'm doing it well, Clint. I really am."

"And what happens if you become president?" Clint asked.

"Jesus," Senator McClain said, cutting off a huge chunk of rare steak and stuffing it into his mouth, "wouldn't that be the biggest con of all?"

# SIXTEEN

The senator's driver was waiting patiently outside when Clint left the restaurant; his head still spinning from the yarn Owen McClain—for that was how he thought of the man—had spun for him. Whether it was true was something he was going to have to decide.

"How was your dinner, sir?"

At that moment Clint realized that he did not know the driver's name and that he wished to.

"What's your name, driver?"

"Henry, sir."

"Well, Henry, the dinner was fine, just fine—and it was very informative."

"I'm happy to hear that, sir. Are we ready to go?"

Very little had passed between the two men once the meal was started—and it had been a very good meal.

"Yes, Henry," he said, climbing aboard the carriage, "we are ready to go."

Owen McClain had made it very clear that it was all up to Clint now. He could either expose him or stand by quietly and watch how far this con man went in the United States government.

Hell, Clint thought, that would just put him with lots of other con men.

When Clint arrived at the Denver House Hotel, his intention was to walk straight through the lobby and up to his room, but when he was halfway to the stairs, the clerk looked up, saw him, and motioned him over. It was the same man he had spoken to about all of the people checking out.

"A message for you, sir," the man said. He turned and took a piece of folded paper out of Clint's box and handed it to him.

"I was asked to make sure you got it before you went up to your room."

"All right, thank you."

He debated reading it right there and then decided to go to his room instead.

He had fitted his key into the lock when he heard something from inside the room, possibly the scrape of a foot along the floor. Never hesitating, lest he give away the fact that he had heard, he turned the key with his left hand and entered the room with his right hand near his gun.

He spotted someone by the window, silhouetted by the moonlight, and made the near fatal mistake of assuming he was alone. By the time he realized his error, a man who had been behind the door stepped out and wrapped powerful arms around him in a bear hug.

Arms pinned at his side, he was unable to reach his gun. The man by the window started for him and he knew he was in for a beating unless he did something fast.

With all the strength he could muster from his legs, he drove himself backward, carrying the man with him. As the man's back came in contact with the wall, the air *whooshed* out of his lungs onto the back of Clint's neck, and his hold weakened.

Clint broke the hold just as the other man reached them and was preparing to throw a punch. He jabbed the man in the face and followed with a right to the body. The man groaned and folded up. Clint turned to face the other man, who had recovered quicker than he hoped. Clint was struck with a body blow and groaned, just as the first man had done seconds before. He did not fold up, however, because that would have left him helpless. Instead he staggered, attempting to keep his feet, but in the attempt he tripped over the first man and fell sprawling to the floor.

The first kick caught him on the right side, the second on the left shoulder. They were coming from two directions after that, and after a few more blows he really didn't feel anything at all . . .

When he woke up, his first thought was that he was glad he was able to wake up. Obviously, they had not been out to kill him, or they would have while he was helpless.

He climbed painfully to his feet, staggered, and landed on the bed, which he decided was comfortable enough to go to sleep on.

Later he woke and decided to wash up. He stood up carefully, walked to the pitcher and basin on the dresser next to the window, and filled the basin with water. Taking off his shirt was a painful experience, but he finally got it off and wet down his face and chest. Drying off, he wondered idly if he had walked in on two men ransacking his room looking for something to steal—although the room didn't look particularly ransacked—or if the attack had had something to do with the two murders and the fact that he was investigating them. If that were the case, then he was surprised that the two men had not tried to impart some kind of message to him, instead of merely leaving him battered and bruised on the floor.

After he'd dried off, he remembered the message in his shirt pocket. He opened it, read it, checked out the name in some surprise, and then read it again.

The author of the note wanted him to meet with her the following evening for dinner, and two points in particular about the note intrigued him.

The first was the meeting place. It was the same restaurant he'd just had dinner at with Owen McClain, alias Senator Alvin McCloud.

The second point was the name of the person who had written the note. It was from Mrs. Dorothy Chandler.

# SEVENTEEN

Getting out of bed in the morning was an adventure. He could feel the toes of his attackers' boots with every move he made, and he was trying to decide whether or not to tell Ellie Lennox about it when there was a knock on his door.

He shuffled to the door and opened it. Ellie barged past him into the room, and then he turned to regard her with her hands on her hips.

"Good morning to you, too," he said.

"I followed you last night."

"Really?" He was truly surprised at her statement. It had never even occurred to him that she'd do that. "Why?"

"Because there's something you're not telling me."

"Like what?"

She was still unaware of his injuries because he hadn't yet moved from in front of the door.

He was as surprised at her appearing as he was at her statement because he hadn't even had a chance to address the question of whether or not to tell her about Owen McClain.

Now he was being forced into a decision, unless he could turn the tables on her.

"What right have you got to follow me, anyway?" he

demanded, contriving to sound indignant. "Did you think I
was going to meet a woman?"

"Even if you were it wouldn't matter a damn to me, Clint
Adams—" She broke off abruptly because he had chosen
that moment to move, and it was very obvious that he was not
moving well.

"What happened to you?"

"You were following me last night," he said, moving to
where his gunbelt was. "Can't you tell me?"

"I followed you to the restaurant where you had dinner
with Senator McCloud. I didn't follow you after that because
I assumed you were coming back here."

"I did and I had company."

He explained what happened to him after he entered his
room, and she expressed concern about his health. "Maybe
you should see a doctor."

"That's not necessary," he said, strapping on his gun.
"I've been bruised before."

"All right, then," she said. "Tell me why you went to see
Senator McCloud."

"Would it do any good to tell you that it was a private
matter and has no bearing on this case?"

"Like spitting in the wind."

"That's what I was afraid of."

"Come on, Clint, we're working together."

"Let's get something straight, first," he said. "If I tell you
something in the strictest confidence, would you feel bound
by that?"

"Of course."

"Even if what I told you . . . bent the law a little?"

"You have to bend the law a little to catch lawbreakers,
Clint," she said patiently, "because they're bending it a
whole lot."

"All right, then," he said. "Here it is. I knew Senator

Alvin McCloud before he became a senator. In fact, before he went into politics.''

"I knew it!'' she said. "I knew there was a flash of recognition in his eyes when he saw you.''

She was good, he thought. He was becoming more and more impressed with her as a detective and as a woman.

"Who was he?''

"Whoever he was he wasn't always honest.''

"Hell, he's a politician now,'' she said. "How less honest can he be now than he was then?''

"I don't know what his reputation is now—''

"It's good,'' she interjected with some reluctance.

"Then his past doesn't matter.''

"Unless he's wanted for murder or something equally as heinous.''

"He's not,'' Clint said. "You can take my word for that.''

"Is Alvin McCloud his real name?''

Clint didn't answer immediately.

"This *is* in strict confidence, isn't it?'' she asked.

"There are still things I don't feel privileged to tell you, Ellie. The man seems to have turned his life around—''

"Are you suggesting we wipe him off as a suspect?''

"No, but I am suggesting that we judge him on his present and not his past.''

"What if I put the question to him?''

"If he wants to answer you, that's up to him.''

"Did he ask you if you were going to expose him?''

"No. He said that whether I did or not was up to me, and he would watch the newspapers to find out what my decision was.''

"He didn't threaten you?''

"No.''

"And he was alone at dinner, right? I mean, I saw no one else but his driver.''

"He was alone."

"He's a politician," she said, "and I have this ingrown distrust of politicians."

"You're not alone there."

"But you're vouching for him?"

"I am."

She frowned and asked, "Were you friends?"

"Not exactly. I had some respect for him then. I think I have more for him now."

She remained silent for a few moments and he found that he couldn't predict what her reply would be to all of this.

"All right," she said. "I'll respect you on this and take your word for it."

"Thank you. If we find something to implicate him in the murders, I'll be the first one to brace him on it."

"I'll agree to go along on one condition."

"What's that?"

"That you let me take you to a doctor now, this morning."

"Just like a woman," he said. "Devious to the end."

"Is it a deal?"

"After breakfast?" he asked.

She sighed and said, "All right, after breakfast."

The doctor—one of Ellie's choice, since Clint did not know one in Denver—told Clint that he probably had a cracked rib, but there was nothing that could be done about it.

"It has to heal itself," young Dr. Kanaly said.

"Thanks a lot, Doc," Clint replied. "What do I owe you?"

"Nothing," Kanaly said. "This was a favor for Ellie."

It was then that Clint realized that the young doctor—with his blond hair, blue eyes and firm, cleft chin—had it bad for Ellie Lennox.

"What did he say?" she asked as he exited the office.

"I'm fine, but I'm sure he'd like to tell you about it over dinner."

"He's a sweet boy."

The sweet boy was at least thirty, which was at least five years older than Ellie. It was obvious that Ellie did not reciprocate the man's feelings. For some reason, Clint found himself feeling pleased about that.

"You'd know better than me," he said, finishing buttoning his shirt. He felt a twinge, but it was bearable. Maybe he didn't have a cracked rib, after all.

"Are we going to see the senator now?" she asked.

"Without an appointment?"

"I have a feeling we'll get in to see him," she said, touching his arm. "I've got some connections in fairly high places."

Clint nodded and said, "Yeah, we're going to see the senator now."

# EIGHTEEN

Ellie Lennox was right; they did get to see the senator as soon as Clint gave his name to a servant.

"I didn't expect to see you again so soon, Clint," the man said, eyeing Ellie curiously.

"Well, something came up, as you can see."

"Like what? This lovely young lady?"

"This lovely young lady is a damned good detective. She followed me last night to my dinner meeting."

McCloud looked at her again and said, "Oh, I see. And how much did you tell her?"

"Very little, in fact," Ellie said. "Clint said I'd have to get the particulars from you—if you're willing to give them to me, that is."

"And if I'm not willing?"

"Well, he did say I was a damned good detective. I could simply use what he did give me as a start."

The senator looked at Clint for some kind of guidance, and after the Gunsmith nodded, he addressed Ellie.

"All right, young lady, what is it you'd like to know about me?"

"What's your real name?"

"McClain, Owen McClain."

"I never heard of you," she said, frowning. "Are you supposed to be famous or something?"

"In some circles."

"Pinkerton might recognize the name. Some of his older operatives might, too," Clint said.

"What was it you did before you went into politics?" Ellie asked Owen McClain.

"I was a con man."

"And a damned good one," Clint said.

"Hell, I was the best."

Both Clint and McClain watched Ellie closely, waiting for her reaction, and when it came, it did surprise McClain, but not Clint.

"Well," she said, "at least you had good training for your present job."

McClain looked at Clint then, smiled, and said, "I like this lady."

"Me, too," Clint admitted, and Ellie gave him a funny look.

"Would you like some brandy?" he asked both of them.

"Yes," Clint said.

"Please," Ellie said.

As McClain—for that's who he truly was, now, with these two people who knew the truth—poured the brandy, Ellie asked, "Does this mean we're friends?"

"The brandy? It means I like you. We've got to go around and around a whole lot more before we're friends, little lady, but it could happen."

"I don't have any politician friends," she said, accepting the brandy. "It might make for an interesting new experience."

McClain gave Clint his brandy and then carried his own behind his desk.

"What else do you want to know?" he asked Ellie.

"I want to know if you killed your wife and her lover."

Again McClain looked at Clint and smiled before answering her. "You come right to the point, don't you?"

"I want to solve this murder, Mr. McClain—or Senator McCloud, if you prefer."

"Since it's just us," the man said, grinning, "you can call me Owen."

"Owen."

"No, I did not kill my wife and her lover."

"You're playing with words now."

"What do you mean."

"You said that you didn't kill your wife *and* her lover."

"So?" he asked, looking genuinely puzzled.

"That doesn't mean that you didn't kill your wife *or* her lover."

McClain frowned and said, "I don't think I'm that clever."

"I don't doubt it."

"You're saying that I went up there—"

"*Might* have gone up there . . ."

"And maybe killed one or the other, but not both?"

"It's possible."

"And if I killed one, who killed the other?"

"You tell me."

Getting into the spirit of the game now, Owen McClain said, "How about Dorothy Chandler. Wait, I've got it," he said, holding up his hands before she could say anything. "Dorothy and I were having an affair and wanted to be rid of our spouses, so we made a pact and went up there and killed them."

"Who killed who?" Clint asked.

"Does it matter?" McClain asked. "Wait, maybe it does.

I know! I killed her husband and she killed my wife. It's downright poetic!'' He looked at Ellie and asked, ''What do you think? Does it work?''

''It can.''

''Except for one thing.''

''What?''

''I did not kill anyone.''

''Well, hell,'' Ellie said, ''why didn't you say so in the first place?''


''What do you think?'' Clint asked Ellie as they left the senator's house—and whatever his name was, he certainly was a senator. They couldn't take that away from him—not at that moment, anyway.

''I like him a lot better as Owen McClain than I do as Alvin McCloud.

''What about that story he told you?'' Clint asked, refer- ring to the story of how Owen McClain became Alvin McCloud.''

''I don't have any problem with that.''

''What do you have a problem with?''

''Liking him, for one thing,'' she said.

''Why's that a problem?''

''I'm just not used to liking politicians.''

''Well, console yourself with the thought that it's the con man you like, not the politician.''

''Was he?''

''Was he what?''

''Being a con man?''

''He's always being a con man, but I don't think he was conning us—not about how he got here, anyway.''

''What about the murders?'' she asked. ''Do you think he did either or both?''

''No.''

"Why?"

"Instinct. I just don't think he's a murderer."

"Neither do I. Where does that leave us?"

"With my dinner date tonight."

"You have a dinner date tonight? With who?"

"Dorothy Chandler."

"How did that happen?"

"I don't know. I guess she must have been impressed with me. She sent me a note that she'll be sending a carriage for me tonight."

"My, aren't we popular!" Ellie said sarcastically. "Everyone is sending a carriage for you these days."

"Well, there's one consolation for you."

"What's that?"

"You won't have to follow me," he said. "You know where I'm going."

# NINETEEN

"Do you know how old I am?"

The question was coming from Dorothy Chandler, who was seated across from him at a table in the dining room of her house. Upon his arrival and after being shown in by her butler, he had been surprised to find out that they would be dining in. He was not naive enough to think that she was doing the cooking, however, and he was right.

Dinner had been served, and they were on dessert when the question came. Up to then, small talk had prevailed, and he still had not discovered why she had asked him there.

"Excuse me?" he asked, not quite hearing her question.

"My age," Dorothy Chandler said, "do you know it?"

"I'm sorry, no, I don't."

"Could you guess it?"

He probably could, and then she'd get insulted. His estimate stood at forty-eight, but then he could always shave a few years off it to make her feel good, only he didn't feel like playing that game.

"Why don't you just tell me?"

"You don't want to guess?"

"No. I would either lie to you or insult you, and I don't want to do either."

"I see," she said. She stopped eating her dessert and folded her hands in her lap. "You don't like games."

"No, I don't."

"Then I guess you'd like me to tell you why I invited you here?"

"Very much."

"It's very simple, really. I want to go to bed with you."

"Mrs. Chandler, I'm flattered—"

"Fifty-two."

"What?"

"I'm fifty-two years old."

He had to admit she didn't look it. She was a handsome figure of a woman with dark hair going gray. She was wearing a blue gown that was cut daringly low, and her full, creamy bosom threatened to spill over onto the table. She was either very firm or firmly cinched in.

"You don't look it."

"Which was that?" she asked. "The lie or the insult."

"Neither. That was the truth."

"Then what is your answer?"

"To what?"

"My offer of a bed for the night."

"Mrs. Chandler—"

"Am I too old?"

"No, of course not."

"Then what? Is it that little partner of yours?"

"No."

"Are you married?"

"No."

"Gelded?"

"No! Mrs. Chandler—"

"Call me Dorothy."

"Dorothy—"

"Come on, Clint," she said, standing up. "Let's fuck."

She reached behind her and undid something that caused the entire gown to fall away from her to the floor.

"I have my clothes specially made to do that," she told him.

"And do you do it often?"

"Only with a man I want."

She discarded her underclothing, which was merely functional and not supportive, and stood before him naked.

Damn, but she certainly didn't look like a fifty-two-year-old woman!

Her breasts were firm and large and sagging only slightly, but he felt that was more from their weight than a matter of her age. Women built as she was always had breasts with a slight sag to them, but that was fine. It made their breasts slightly pendulous, which came in handy when the woman was on top.

"I can tell you're interested," she said, moving to his side of the table, "but let's see how interested."

She leaned over and put one hand to his crotch. Her breasts brushed his face. The valley between them was fragrant, and her brown nipples were hard and distended. They brushed across his face and, almost involuntarily, his tongue flicked out to taste them.

At the same time, she found his penis hard and ready, and she said, "Oh, you are interested, aren't you?"

"Damn it," he growled, standing up, "I told you I don't like games."

He pulled her to him and kissed her soundly. She moaned and thrust her tongue into his mouth. The kiss went on for a long time and was broken by him, for it seemed that she could have gone on forever without taking a breath.

They were both breathless, however, and he took her in his

arms and lifted her from the floor. She was a heavy woman, but he was able to handle her.

"Where's the damned bedroom?"

She pointed.

"Did you kill them, Dorothy?"

She gave him a surprised look from her side of the four-poster and said, "You can ask me that after what we just did? Didn't I come across as loving, darling?"

"Demanding is more like it."

"Well," she said, reaching for and fondling his semi-erect penis, "you certainly had no trouble meeting the demand, did you?"

"You're changing the subject."

"Is that why you came here tonight?" she asked. "To ask me that?"

"I came here tonight because you asked me to, remember?"

"Oh, I remember, darling."

"And you must have known this subject would come up."

"I thought I might be able to distract you," she said, fondling him with a little more insistence now. He could feel himself stiffening in her hand.

"You did, and you may still, but I'd like an answer to the question without any sort of word games attached. Did you kill them?"

"No," she said, "I did not."

"Any idea who did?"

"You and your partner asked me that already."

"I thought you might have a different answer this time."

"I don't," she said, running her fingernails up and down the underside of his now fully erect cock. She shivered involuntarily.

''I don't know who killed them, and I don't particularly care,'' she said, ''especially at this moment.''

She slithered down so that she could replace her nails with her tongue, and she began licking his length avidly. Hefting his balls, she then took him into her mouth.

She was probably like no other fifty-two-year-old woman in the world.

# TWENTY

He was prepared for Ellie Lennox's onslaught. He had accepted the fact that there was an attraction between them, one that neither of them was quite willing to do anything about yet, but it was enough of an attraction so that they argued like an old married couple every chance they got.

When he left Dorothy Chandler's house, he went back to his hotel, where he expected Ellie to be waiting for him in his room. Instead, she confronted him in front of the hotel. Luckily, it was late and there were few people on the street.

"It took you that long to dine and talk to her, huh?" she demanded. "Just talk, is that what you're going to tell me?"

"Why do I have to tell you anything?" he asked. "We're only partners, Ellie; we're not married. And we're only temporary partners."

"Well, thank God for that," she said. "I'd hate to have to wait around for you day in and day out while you go to bed with every female suspect we have to question."

He really had no defense against that. He didn't have to go to bed with Dorothy Chandler and probably not with Amanda Foxworth, either, but he wasn't the kind of man who could just turn a beautiful, willing woman down. It was his nature to enjoy women—and to give them enjoyment—and if it didn't hurt anyone, where was the harm?

He knew Ellie Lennox could never accept logic like that, though.

"Look," he said, "I don't want to argue about this, especially not out here on the street."

"Oh, I get it," she said. "You want to get me up to your room. Maybe you think you can get me into bed, too, huh? Haven't you had enough tonight? Or even this week?"

"The thought never entered my mind, Ellie."

She didn't take that well, either.

"Oh? And why not? Don't you think I'd be any good in bed? Or as good as Amanda or Dorothy Chandler?"

"We're supposed to be discussing this case, Ellie," he reminded her, "not each other's loves."

"Fine," she said, putting her hands on her hips, "fine. Go ahead, discuss."

"I think maybe this should wait until tomorrow when you've calmed down."

"I'm calm," she said irritably, "I'm very calm."

"Ellie."

She hit him with her fist then and let it bounce harmlessly off his shoulder. "I'm calm!" she snapped.

"Ellie—" he said, reaching for her.

"Don't touch me, Clint."

"Go home," he said, pulling his hands back. "Think about what you've said tonight. In the morning, if you still want to work with me, come back. All right?"

She opened her mouth as if to respond and then abruptly closed it again. When she finally did speak, she really did sound calm. "You won't leave?"

"I'll be here, waiting."

"All right," she said, backing away from him. "All right, I'll go home and think about it."

''Good.''

''I still think it stinks,'' she said, ''but I'll think about it.''

''That's all I ask.''

''You big bastard,'' she said and then turned on her heels and walked away.

Damn it, but he liked her, even if she was a pain in the neck sometimes. She was exactly the kind of woman he could never marry, for she would be possessive and jealous and hell to live with.

But he liked her.

After Clint left Dorothy Chandler's house, the woman got dressed for her meeting with Senator Alvin McCloud.

Downstairs she said to Hirsch, ''Have my carriage brought around.''

''Very good, madam.''

When the carriage was out front, she said, ''Hirsch, you're sure the senator received my message to meet me?''

''He did, madam.''

''And he'll be there?''

''Yes.''

''Alone?''

''Madam—''

''Never mind,'' she said with impatience. ''I'll find all of that out when I get there, won't I?''

''Yes, madam.''

''Have some tea ready for me when I return, Hirsch,'' she said. ''I shouldn't be more than an hour.''

''Yes, madam.''

When she left, neither of them had any way of knowing just how long she really would be gone.

Clint returned to his room, dissatisfied at some of the aspects of his meeting with Dorothy Chandler. She had never really told him why she wanted to see him—unless taking him to bed was the actual reason, but he found that hard to accept. He was attractive to women, he knew that, but still there must have been another reason, one which she had decided not to broach with him.

He decided to approach her again the next day and find out what it was rather than return to her house tonight.

What difference could twelve hours or so make?

# TWENTY-ONE

Clint was awakened the next morning by an insistent knocking at his door. He stumbled out of bed and to the door in his underwear, assuming that it was Ellie.

The two uniformed policeman at the door stared at him when he opened it. One of them asked, "Clint Adams?"

"That's right."

"Would you come with us, please?"

"What for?"

"We're with the police department, sir. Our superior, Lieutenant Gorman, would like to speak with you."

"About what?"

"He'll tell you that, sir."

"Where?"

"He's waiting for you at Mr. Pinkerton's office."

"Why at Pinkerton's—" he started to ask, then stopped short, and said, "Never mind. You wouldn't know that either, would you?"

"No, sir."

"All right, just let me get dressed."

"We wish you would, sir."

Clint squinted at the two of them, searching for a trace of

humor, but they were both straightfaced, so he shut the door
and proceeded to get dressed.

When he entered Pinkerton's office, the old man was
seated behind his desk, and seated across from him was a
gray-haired man in his forties who stood up, grunting from
the effort it took to lift his sturdy bulk.

"Mr. Adams?" the man asked.

"That's right."

"I'm Lieutenant Gorman, sir. I'd like to ask you a few
questions."

"About what?"

Gorman looked past him at the two policemen and said,
"That'll be all."

The only other person in the room, seated in a corner, was
Ellie Lennox, but he was unable to tell anything from the look
on her face.

"About what?" Clint asked again.

"Mr. Adams, I understand that you saw Mrs. Dorothy
Chandler last evening?"

It was less a question than a statement, but Clint responded
by saying, "Yes, that's right. Why?"

"Well, sir, she's dead this morning, and you seem to be
the last person to have seen her alive."

"Except for her man," Clint said immediately.

"Well, yes, except for her man," the lieutenant agreed.
"He's the one who told us about you."

"Naturally."

"Now, as I understand it," Gorman said, "you work for
Mr. Pinkerton—"

"I don't actually work for him—"

"Oh?" Gorman said, looking first at Pinkerton and then
back to Clint. "If that's the truth, then you've been hindering

a police investigation, Mr. Adams. If you were doing your investigating without any sort of official standing, I'd be forced to address you.''

''You're absolutely right,'' Clint said, ''I work for Mr. Pinkerton.''

''On a temporary basis,'' Pinkerton interjected.

''Well, that doesn't matter,'' Gorman said, ''as long as he's on your payroll at this time.''

Pinkerton looked at Clint and then said, ''Yes, he is.''

''Well, good,'' Gorman said, looking at Clint again. ''Then we don't have to worry about that.''

''Good,'' Clint said.

''Now, Mr. Adams, would you relate to me the nature of any conversation you might have had with Mrs. Chandler last night?''

''All of it?''

''Of course,'' Gorman said. ''There's no telling what part of it might help us.''

''How was she killed?'' Clint asked. ''Where?''

''Mr. Adams,'' the lieutenant said, ''we would get much further if you would answer my questions first. After that, well, perhaps I can answer some of yours. Agreed?''

Clint nodded and began to talk, telling the policeman what he and Dorothy had talked about last night—leaving out the fact that some of the conversation had taken place in her bed.

''Is that all of it?'' Gorman asked when Clint stopped talking.

''Yes, that's all of it.''

''And when you left, did she indicate to you that she might be going out?''

''No, not at all,'' Clint said. Before he could stop himself, he added, ''She was in bed.''

He saw Pinkerton wince and Ellie put her hand to her

forehead, but Gorman took it in stride.

"Indeed? Then she must have gotten dressed and left after you did."

"Her man must have told you that."

"Oh, yes, he did, he did," Gorman said absently. "I just wanted to hear it from you."

The policeman stood there then, partially bent over with one hand on his lower back as if it hurt him and the other hand to his forehead as if he were concentrating mightily on something.

"Lieutenant?" Clint said, trying to attract the man's attention.

"Hmmm?" Gorman said, as if started from a reverie. "Oh, I'm sorry. I was just trying to sort the facts out in my mind. I like to do that. It helps me to concentrate."

"I'm sure," Clint said, entertaining sudden doubts about the man's competency.

"All right, well, I guess that's it, then," Gorman said, turning to Pinkerton. "Thank you for your cooperation, Mr. Pinkerton."

"Of course," Pinkerton said, shaking hands with the man. "My people are always at your disposal."

"Thank you," Gorman said again. He then turned to face Ellie and said, "And thank you, miss."

Ellie merely inclined her head, and Gorman turned to face Clint.

"Lieutenant, you said you'd answer my questions after I answered yours."

"Did I say that?" the man said, frowning as if he couldn't remember.

"You did."

The man put his right hand to his forehead again, standing in that odd bent position, and said, "I thought I said I *might* answer your questions.''

"Well, yes," Clint admitted, "you did, but—"

"Well, all right," Lieutenant Gorman said, cutting Clint off, "I suppose there's no harm. What were your questions, again?"

"How and where did she die?"

"Oh, she had been stabbed repeatedly and was found in an alley off Delancey Street. That street name wouldn't ring a bell with you, would it?"

"I'm afraid it doesn't. I don't know Denver very well.''

"Well, I do, but I don't know what a society lady like her was doing over there. My wife, she tells me that rich people usually stay in their own end of town, but I guess she's wrong, my wife. She'll be disappointed to find that out.''

"I guess so," Clint said, a bit puzzled by the man. Why was he talking about his wife?

"Well, that's all, then. I'd appreciate it, Mr. Adams, if you'd make an effort not to leave town for a while.''

"I hadn't intended to.''

"Fine, fine, then I'm not interfering with any travel plans of yours, am I?"

"Not at all.''

"Good.'' Gorman moved toward the door and said, "I guess I have everything I need.''

He opened the door, started through it, and then suddenly stopped and turned, executing that hand-to-head, bent position again.

"One more thing.''

"What's that?" Clint asked.

"Uh, what was it?—oh, yes. Did you believe Dorothy Chandler, Mr. Adams, when she said she didn't care who killed her husband and Senator McCloud's wife?''

"Yes, I did."

"I see."

"Do you see any connection between her death and her husband's?"

"Well, the only connection at the moment is that they were both stabbed to death during the same week. Other than that," he said, raising his arms and then letting them fall heavily to his sides, "I'm puzzled. Good-bye to you all."

After the man left, Clint turned to look at both Ellie and Pinkerton.

Pinkerton, noticing the puzzled look on Clint's face, said, "Don't underestimate that man."

"You mean it's an act?"

Pinkerton nodded and said, "He's a very good detective. I've often asked him to quit the police force and come to work for me, but like you, he refuses."

"Speaking of which—"

"Don't thank me for keeping you out of jail," Pinkerton said, holding up one hand. "You're working with one of my people, which means that, though indirectly, you are working for me."

"Am I working with one of your people?" Clint asked, looking at Ellie in the corner.

It was Pinkerton's turn to frown now and he looked at Ellie and asked, "Is there some problem, Miss Lennox?"

"No, sir," she said, pushing away from the corner. "No problem at all, sir. Come on, Clint," she said, tugging at the Gunsmith's arm, "we've got work to do."

"You certainly have, Miss Lennox," Pinkerton said. "You now have three murders to solve if you want to keep your job."

"Don't worry, sir," she said with confidence, "we'll solve them."

Clint wished he felt as confident as she did. If they could keep from fighting each other long enough, she might be right.

# TWENTY-TWO

"They're connected," Ellie said when they were in the hall.

"You think so?"

"He thinks so," she said, jerking her thumb at Pinkerton's door, "and so do I."

"Poor Dorothy Chandler," Clint said. "I never met a woman who was so proud of her age and now she won't be getting any older."

"How old did she tell you she was?" Ellie asked.

"Fifty-two."

"Are you always so gullible?" she asked. "She was forty-eight, but she thought she'd look better to people if she lied and said she was older."

"She was right."

She gave him a look and started down the hall. Coming the other way, George Brigham tried to intercept her.

"Ellie, I want to talk to you—"

"Can't, George. I'm busy," she said, sweeping past him.

"Miss Lennox," he snapped, grabbing her arm, "you're forgetting who your boss is!"

Clint was about to step in when Ellie jerked her arm loose and said, "George, why don't you drop dead?"

Brigham's mouth fell open as she continued on down the hall and Clint moved past him, smiling broadly.

Amanda Foxworth watched angrily as Clint Adams and Ellie Lennox left Pinkerton's office. Amanda was aware that Dorothy Chandler had been killed, and she was annoyed that she had not been made privy to the meeting that had just taken place with Pinkerton, Adams, Ellie, and the police. She felt that an attempt was being made to make her look bad by helping Ellie Lennox solve the case. Why else would Pinkerton himself have called her in?

She decided that she would take her anger out on poor George Brigham. In addition to letting off some steam, there might be something the pathetic man could tell her that would possibly help her.

Idly, as she approached Brigham's office, she wondered where her partner was and what he was doing?

Poor Dorothy Chandler, the man thought. For a woman many men would have considered old, she was really re-markable, in and out of bed. Out of bed, however, she did have a tendency to talk too much.

Dorothy Chandler was history now, however, and the man—the killer—turned his mind toward problems of a more immediate nature.

The Pinkertons.

And Clint Adams.

Although the Pinkertons were trained detectives and Clint Adams was not, the killer felt that the Gunsmith was far and away the biggest threat. It was too bad that the two burglars—who had turned out to be bunglers—had not killed him, but then that was asking coincidence to step in rather easily.

No, if he wanted the threat of Clint Adams removed, the killer was going to have to remove it himself.

"This narrows it down, you know," Ellie Lennox said to Clint.

It had been Ellie's suggestion that they go to her place to discuss the case, since she lived so nearby. She had two rooms above a restaurant which she had told him—just in passing—had terrible food, but good coffee. Clint suggested that he might like to sample that coffee, and she simply shrugged her shoulders and agreed.

Now, across the table from him, she said, "You know that it's narrowed now, don't you?"

"You're talking about the senator?"

"Who else?"

"I don't know," he said. "That's what we're supposed to be finding out, isn't it?"

"I know he's your friend, Clint, but he certainly looks more suspicious now than he did before."

"Why? Because he's the easiest mark now that Dorothy Chandler's dead? What if she had hired someone to kill her husband and Mrs. McCloud and then refused to pay him?"

"And he killed her?"

"It's just an example of how other possibilities do exist."

Reluctantly Ellie said, "Yeah, I guess it could have happened that way, but I think we should talk to Senator McCloud again."

"There are a lot of other people we could talk to."

"Yeah? Name one?"

Clint was ready for that. "Dorothy's servant, Hirsch."

"What could he tell us?"

"Who she's been sleeping with, for one. That would probably give us a list of suspects."

"Present company included?" she asked.

"If you want to get technical," he responded.

"All right, never mind that," she said, shaking her head. "You're right. We should talk to Hirsch."

"And we should talk to some of her society friends. There may be someone there who wanted her dead for some reason or other."

"And her husband? And the senator's wife?" she said doubtfully.

"Let's not assume that Dorothy's death is definitely related to theirs," Clint warned.

"How could it not be? It's just too much of a coincidence."

"All right, I don't believe in coincidence either—most of the time. But it could be that she was killed during a robbery. All I'm saying is that we should keep an open mind about it."

"Every instinct I have as a detective tells me that all three murders were committed by the same person."

"Too bad your instinct can't tell us exactly who that person is."

"It's giving me a pretty good idea, though."

"Don't start that again—"

"Okay, but there's one other reason we should talk to the senator."

"What's that?"

"The street she was found on."

"Delaney Street? What about it?"

"Like you said to Gorman, you don't know Denver or you would have recognized the street name."

"Why?"

"It's one of your friend's favorite streets," she said. "That's where the restaurant you and he spoke in is."

Clint stared at her and then said, "Sonofabitch! Let's go and talk to the man."

# TWENTY-THREE

The reaction of Senator Alvin McCloud was not what Clint Adams or Ellie Lennox expected. He was, to say the least, somewhat amused at their appearance in his house so soon after Dorothy Chandler's death.

"Come on, Clint," the senator said from behind his desk, before either of them could utter a word. "You mean now that old Dorothy is gone you're just going to settle for me?"

"Nobody said anything about settling, Owen."

"What was she doing on Delaney Street?" Ellie asked, charging full speed ahead. "She wouldn't have been there by any chance to meet you? In a favorite little restaurant of yours?"

The senator looked from Clint to Ellie and then back to Clint. "Sharp little partner you've got here, Clint."

"Then she did meet you?" Clint asked.

"She was *supposed* to meet me," the man corrected him, "but she never showed up. I waited about an hour and then left. You can check that out," he added, looking directly at Ellie.

"Who set up the meeting?" Ellie asked.

"She did. She had sent her driver around with a request that I meet her there."

"Why there?" Clint asked.

"We've, uh, met there before."

"Senator," Ellie said, her tone one of reproach, "don't tell me you were having an affair with the wife of the man who was having an affair with your wife?"

"Yes, that's the way it was. We had"—he seemed at a loss as to what to call what they had and finally settled on "a relationship."

"How did that come about?" Clint asked.

"When Dorothy and I found out about the affair that was going on behind our backs, we met to discuss it. We found out that neither one of us really cared, as long as it was kept reasonably quiet."

"You also found out that you were interested in each other," Ellie added.

"Well, for my part, at least, it was purely physical. I couldn't stand the woman out of bed, but between the sheets she was really remarkable for someone her age."

His words and tone were calculated to embarrass Ellie, but she stared stonily at him, disappointing him.

"Was this still going on of late?" Clint asked.

"No, I called it off weeks ago."

"What did she want to meet you about last night?"

"I don't know," the senator said. "I told you that she never showed up and I left."

"Didn't you bother to look for her?" Ellie asked.

"No," he replied. "She wasn't my responsibility. For all I knew, she could have met someone interesting on the way and got distracted."

"If it were all over, what made you agree to meet her?" Clint asked.

"She said—through her driver, that is—that she wanted to talk about the murders. The indication was that she knew something."

"Do you think she really did, or was she trying to rekindle the flame?"

"Dorothy rekindle the flame? Believe me, Clint, it was no great romance that we had. When I called it off, she just went on to the next poor fella. No, if she wanted to see me it was because she knew something."

Clint wondered, if Dorothy were still alive and he broached the subject of her relationship with the senator, who she would say called it off.

"And it got her killed," Ellie said.

"That's a shame. Do you think it was the same person— wait, of course you do," he said, as if suddenly struck by a revelation. "That's why you're here, to try to hang it on me."

"Nobody's trying to hang anything on you, Owen," Clint assured him.

"Oh, no? Believe me, a lot of people are trying to hang me, Clint," the man replied. "It's the nature of politics."

"Do you think the murders were committed to try to hurt you?"

"I'd hate to think that three people were killed for that reason," the senator said. "I'd feel awfully guilty about not feeling any particular sense of loss."

Ellie Lennox had her doubts about just how guilty the senator would feel.

"And your campaign?" Ellie asked.

"I told you before. The sympathy vote carries just as much weight as any other."

"Senator, how many of your people knew you were meeting Dorothy Chandler last night?"

"My driver."

"That's all?"

"Yes."

"Your campaign manager—"

"Didn't know anything about it."

Ellie and Clint exchanged glances and Clint said, "All right, thanks for seeing us."

"I really had nothing to do with all of this, Clint," Senator McCloud said as they moved toward the door. "I'm an innocent bystander."

"I'd never call you that," Clint said, "but I know what you're trying to say."

"He gave himself a stronger motive," Ellie said outside. "In fact, he's said it more than once."

"What do you mean?"

"The sympathy vote."

"You think he killed his wife and her lover in order to gain more votes?"

"It's possible. You heard him say that their deaths will help him more than hurt him."

"And what about Dorothy's death? What did he gain by murdering her?"

"Well, like you said, maybe it's unrelated—or maybe they did meet last night."

"And she told him she knew and he killed her to keep her quiet."

"Right."

"But in killing her he makes himself the prime suspect in the first two murders—and what if she really did kill them or have them killed? He could end up hanging for something he didn't do."

"You're starting to confuse the hell out of me," Ellie said.

"All right, let's just keep that one on the side for a while," he suggested. "I want to talk to Hirsch."

"What about?"

"He certainly didn't bother keeping my name a secret from the police, but he doesn't seem to have mentioned the senator's planned meeting with his employer last night.''

''Maybe he didn't know.''

''Oh, I think he knew,'' Clint said. ''I'm just curious about what other names he might have kept to himself.''

# TWENTY-FOUR

Despite the demise of his mistress, Hirsch was still living in the Chandler house. He answered the door and regarded Clint and Ellie without surprise. He was as neat as he was when Dorothy Chandler was still alive.

"Yes?"

"We'd like to ask you some questions, Hirsch," Clint said.

"I've already spoken to the police."

"These are questions you might not have answered for them." It was a fine way of telling the man he may have kept something back.

"Very well," the old man said, stepping back. "You may come in."

They stepped inside and waited while Hirsch locked the door and then followed him to the den. Clint didn't know what he'd expected. Perhaps to find the man enjoying his late employer's food and wine, but the house was spotless, as if Hirsch were expecting a surprise inspection from a ghost.

"Please ask your questions and leave," Hirsch said. "I have a lot of work to do."

"Are you getting paid, Hirsch? By Mrs. Chandler's estate, perhaps?"

"I prefer to leave the premises clean when I take my leave and begin to search for other employment," the man explained.

"Do you think Mrs. Chandler might have provided for you in her will, Hirsch?" Ellie asked.

The old man's lined face remained expressionless. "I'm sure I have no idea what is in madam's will. Please, are these the questions you came here to ask?"

"No, Hirsch, they're not," Clint said. "I want to know who Mrs. Chandler was seeing at the time of her death."

"Seeing?"

"Don't play dumb, Hirsch," Ellie said. "Who was she sleeping with."

With that Hirsch gave Clint a very pointed look, which seemed to make Ellie uncomfortable for some reason.

"We know about Mrs. Adams, Hirsch," she snapped, "and about Senator McCloud."

"That had been over for some time."

"She left here to meet him last night, didn't she?"

The old man hesitated just a split second before saying, "Yes."

"Why didn't you tell that to the police?"

Hirsch shrugged.

"You were quick enough to give them my name."

"You are not a state senator, sir."

"Are you thinking that Senator McCloud might reward you in some way for keeping his name to yourself?" Clint asked.

"What the senator does is his business."

"What's your business, Hirsch?" Clint asked. "What have you got in mind? A little blackmail, maybe?"

"You offend me, sir."

"Maybe," Clint said, "and maybe not. But I want some

names right now, Hirsch, or I'm going to do more than offend you."

"Are you threatening me with physical violence, sir?" the elderly man asked.

"If he's not," Ellie said quickly, "I am."

Hirsch looked them both over solemnly and then recited three names.

"Damned nice of you to be so helpful, Hirsch," Clint said. "Would you like to show us to the door?"

"I'm sure you remember the way, sir."

"Yeah, I'm sure we do."

Outside Ellie asked, "Do you really think he was planning on blackmailing the senator?"

"I don't know. What do you think of the three names he gave us?"

"I'm not surprised at one of them," Ellie said. "We all know that Ken Sapir would fuck a snake if someone held its head still."

"What about the second name?"

"I don't know it."

"I do," Clint said. "Jeff Sweet is a killer."

"With a name like that?"

"It's his way of overcoming it."

"Is he good?"

"He's very good."

"But if he were sleeping with her, why would he kill her?"

"Maybe he didn't kill her," Clint suggested. "Maybe he just killed for her."

"I guess the only way to find that out is to find Mr. Sweet."

"Right."

"Do you know him?"

"I know him," Clint said, "and he knows me, which might make it a little hard for me to get near him."

"Why?" she asked. "I thought killers were always out for your reputation?"

"Not Sweet," Clint said. "He's got enough of a reputation of his own without wanting to add to it."

"Then I guess I'll have to talk to him."

"We'll worry about who talks to him after we find him."

"All right, and what about the third name?" Ellie asked.

"Now, that one is a shocker," Clint said. "That's not someone I would expect to find stepping into the senator's slippers."

"Why not? He's a man, isn't he?"

"Definitely," Clint said, "and Vincent Thurston is a man we've overlooked long enough, I believe."

"So do I," Ellie Lennox said. "So do I."

# TWENTY-FIVE

They went back to Senator McCloud's house, this time looking for Vincent Thurston, and were told by a servant that Mr. Thurston was not in.

"Does he live here?" Clint asked the maid.

"No, sir. He has rooms on Montague Street."

"What number?"

After the girl answered, Clint looked at Ellie who nodded and said, "I know where that is."

"All right, let's go," he said. To the maid he said, "Thank you."

"I'll have to tell the master you were here asking," the black maid said.

"Of course, you will," he said, smiling. She smiled back nervously and closed the door.

"You charmer, you," Ellie said.

"Let's go."

Vincent Thurston did not live where you might think someone involved with a successful politician would live.

"Isn't this a little below his station?" Clint asked.

This section of Denver reminded him very much of the Five Points section of Manhattan, which he had seen when he was in New York recently. The buildings were old and run down, some of them even abandoned. Thurston's building, however, had retained a certain look of fading grandeur, Clint noticed after a second look.

"This used to be an exclusive part of town," Ellie told him.

"Looks like it still is," Clint remarked, "only in a different way."

They approached the building and found that the main floor had once been a gun shop. It had long since been abandoned, but there still seemed to be some stock on hand. Looking in the window, Clint thought that it might be worth a return visit later on, before he left Denver.

They mounted the steps to the second floor where Thurston was supposed to have his rooms. Clint knocked, and when there was no answer, he knocked again.

"Nobody home," he said.

"Let's go in anyway."

"My sentiments exactly."

Ellie backed away and Clint, bracing his back against the opposite wall, kicked out with the heel of his right foot, catching the door just below the knob. Wood splintered and the door crashed open. Clint wondered how they would explain themselves if the man were simply a sound sleeper.

He wasn't asleep, however. He was dead.

"Jesus," Ellie said, standing in the doorway. It was then that Clint saw that she was holding a small derringer in her hand.

"Wait outside, Ellie," Clint said, entering the room carefully.

The man's body was lying across the bed, and the smell of blood filled the room. Clint crouched by the body and found that the bed clothes were soaked with blood beneath the man, whose throat appeared to have been cut. He'd been dead for some time.

"Jesus," Ellie said again, this time from directly behind Clint.

"I told you—" Clint said, but he didn't have to tell her again. She clapped both hands over her mouth and ran for the hallway. Clint could hear her being sick. At least that would keep her occupied for a while.

Clint started a swift, methodical search of the room, not knowing exactly what he was looking for. All he knew was that he wanted a look around before he called Lieutenant Gorman to the scene.

He went through a chest of drawers, finding nothing but some clothing and personal effects of the deceased Mr. Thurston. At least, the man on the bed resembled Thurston. He'd lost so much blood that his face seemed to have fallen in on itself, but he was still recognizable to someone observant.

There was no visible sign of a struggle or of a search. Whoever had killed Thurston had come there with only that specific act in mind.

Clint completed his search of the rest of the room and moved to the small table by the bedside. When he opened the top drawer, he stopped short as he stared at the contents with a mixture of fascination and revulsion.

"What is it?" a voice asked from the doorway.

He looked over his shoulder to see Ellie standing there. Her voice sounded hoarse, a result of all of the retching she'd done in the hall.

"What did you find?"

It took him a few moments to find his voice and then he said, "Fingers."

"What?" she asked, moving cautiously into the room.

"Two fingers, probably from two different people—" He

stopped short when he realized that she was moving toward him.

"Ellie, no—" he said, but it was too late. She looked over his shoulder at the two fingers sitting side by side on a white cloth, and then she was running for the hall again.

With the rasping sounds of her dry heaves behind him, Clint stopped to examine the fingers. It was odd, but finding the fingers had shocked him more than finding Thurston's body. Well, maybe it wasn't so odd, after all. He'd seen so many bodies during his lifetime, but the number of severed fingers he'd come across could be counted on the fingers of one . . .

He was sure that one finger was the index finger of a woman while the other—more blunt and longer and with a shorter fingernail—had belonged to a man.

And he had an idea who the man and woman had been.

# TWENTY-SIX

"That was something we kept out of the papers," Lieutenant Jack Gorman said. Clint and Ellie had had him summoned to the hotel.

"The fingers?" Clint said.

"Yeah," Gorman said. They both moved aside so two men could carry out the body of Vincent Thurston. "When you've worked on as many murders as I have, you find that there are a lot of people willing to confess."

"To something they didn't do?"

Gorman nodded. "Holding back information like this is the only way to tell the nuts from the real killers."

Clint could see the logic in that. If someone confessed and knew nothing about the severed fingers, then it would be obvious that he was not the killer. Something else occurred to him, then. "What about Dorothy Chandler?"

"What about her?"

"Was she missing a finger?"

Gorman looked at Clint and gone was the buffoon he first met at the Pinkerton office. What remained was a sharp police official who was sizing the Gunsmith up before responding to the question.

"No, she had all her fingers."

"Which probably means she was killed by someone other than whoever killed the other two."

"Unless the killer is looking to confuse us."

"And what about Thurston?"

"Well, he's got all his fingers," Gorman said. "In fact, he's got two too many," he said with an odd sense of humor.

"You think he killed the two in the hotel?"

"It's possible," Gorman said, "even likely. The fingers are here."

"And it's unlikely that the killer was carrying them in his pocket when he killed Thurston and decided to leave them behind to implicate him?" Clint wondered aloud.

"When you're dealing with a sick mind, Mr. Adams, nothing is very unlikely, but I must admit that Mr. Thurston looks good for the hotel killing."

"And Dorothy Chandler."

"We've got nothing to tie him to that."

"Now comes the big question." Gorman looked at Clint and nodded.

"Who killed Thurston."

"And why?" Clint added.

Gorman rubbed his hands over his face and said, "I've handled murders before, but never this many in such a short amount of time. They've got to be connected."

"Well, even if we're dealing with two different killers, it could all still be connected."

"Or three killers," Gorman said. "Suppose Thurston killed the first two, someone else killed the Chandler woman, and then a third party killed Thurston."

"That would mean there were still two killers out there. I like a two-killer idea better. Thurston killed the senator's wife and Dorothy Chandler's husband and then, for some reason, Dorothy Chandler herself."

"And then someone killed him."

"Clint—" a hoarse voice called out from behind them.

Both men turned and discovered that they had forgotten Ellie Lennox, who was still out in the hall.

"Miss Lennox, you should go home," Gorman said.

Clint had never seen her looking the way she looked now—small, helpless, frightened.

"I'll take her home," Clint said.

"Why not come by my office afterward?" Gorman said. "We'll talk more and maybe hack this out together."

Clint felt flattered by the offer and said, "I'd like that."

"How do you like your coffee?"

"Strong and black."

"I'll have a pot waiting," the lieutenant said, and they all started down the stairs.

On the street Gorman spoke to a couple of patrolmen he'd had asking questions in the area. When they'd both reported no progress, he looked up and saw Clint walked away with Ellie Lennox leaning on him.

Gorman had read about Clint Adams and had read even more after meeting the man in Pinkerton's office. Reading between the lines and discounting the sensationalism, he had found himself impressed by the man. Now, after their short interaction in the dead man's room, he was even more impressed.

Gorman was known to be the best detective in Denver, but he didn't mind admitting that he needed help on this one— and maybe Clint Adams was the man to supply that help.

Clint took Ellie Lennox back to her room and attempted to leave her at the door.

"Clint, could you come inside?"

He wanted to get to Gorman's office to continue their conversation, but he decided he could afford a few more moments to be sure that Ellie was all right.

"Sure."

They entered and Ellie turned up the lamp in the front room. "I'm sorry," she said.

"For what?"

"For the way I behaved," she said. Then she added bitterly, "Tough detective."

"What happened tonight doesn't mean you're not tough, Ellie."

"Maybe just not as tough as I think, eh?"

"That might be true," he agreed.

"Yes, I guess it is."

She moved toward him then and surprised him by kissing him gently on the lips.

"You've been sweet to me this evening, and it would be very easy for me to fall into bed with you, but it would be for all the wrong reasons. Please wait until I'm in bed before you leave."

"Of course, Ellie."

He waited while she got herself ready for bed, and then he actually tucked her in, pulling the covers up to her chin.

"Maybe another night . . ." she started, but trailed off as if she didn't know quite how to finish the line.

"I know," Clint said, "I know. Sleep well, Ellie. I think we'll get a lot closer tomorrow to bringing this to an end."

She frowned at him and asked, "What do you know?"

"Nothing . . . yet. I'm going to talk to Gorman again tonight, and I'll see you in the morning. I'll come by to pick you up."

"I'll be all right in the morning."

"I know you will," he said. He kissed her on the forehead and said, "Good night."

"Good night, Clint."

Leaving, he knew that she had been right. It would have been very easy for him to have joined her in bed, but the timing was all wrong.

Maybe another night . . .

# TWENTY-SEVEN

When Clint arrived at Lieutenant Gorman's office in Denver's new brick police station, he found Senator Alvin McCloud there. Obviously, Gorman had sent someone to inform the senator of the murder of his campaign manager and aide.

"Clint, what the hell is going on?" McCloud said, unmindful that Gorman was watching them very closely and now felt certain that the two men had known each other before.

"They're telling me that Vincent is not only dead, but a killer, himself."

"I never told you any such thing," Gorman said, interrupting the politician.

"You implied it."

"That's true," Gorman said.

"Well, it's crazy."

"I found the evidence that implicates him," Clint said.

"What evidence?"

Clint explained about the fingers and McCloud turned on Gorman and said, "I know we kept the mutilation out of the newspapers, and I respected your request to tell no one about it."

"We kept it out of the papers for reasons important to the investigation of your wife's death."

"I realize that."

"There was no need for you to know more. Besides, the husband is always a suspect."

McCloud glared at Gorman and then said, "I see."

"I'm sorry to get you out so late in the evening with such bad news, but I thought you'd like to know."

"Yes, of course, I want to know. Is there a connection between this and the murder of Dorothy Chandler?"

"No tangible connection, no," Gorman admitted, "but we believe that all of these killings are related."

"I see," McCloud said again. "Lieutenant, you'll see that I'm kept informed of your progress?"

"Of course."

McCloud turned to Clint, seemed about to say something, but then nodded and left.

"You two knew each other before," Gorman said, wasting no time.

"It has no bearing on the murders," Clint said, not bothering to deny it.

Gorman regarded Clint quietly for a few moments and then said, "I'll take your word on that—for now."

"Where's that coffee you promised me?"

"Coming up."

They went through several pots of coffee as they exchanged ideas and information.

Clint gave Gorman the three names he'd gotten from Hirsch, and he was surprised when Gorman told him that he knew about Jeff Sweet's presence in Denver.

"We've been keeping an eye on him."

"Constantly?"

"As well as we can," Gorman said. "Unfortunately, he knows we're keeping an eye on him, and every so often he manages to lose the man I've got following him.''

"Have your people seen him with Dorothy Chandler?"

"Yes."

"And with anyone else connected with this case? The senator? The senator's wife? Thurston?"

"None of them," Gorman said, "but he was seen in the company of someone else."

"Who?"

"Amanda Foxworth, the other Pinkerton lady."

"What the hell is she doing with him?"

"As far as we can see, it's been strictly pleasure."

"If you knew Sweet the way I do, you'd know that the only thing he does purely for pleasure is kill."

"I've heard as much. Do you think he might be the one who did all these killings?"

"He's certainly qualified," Clint said, "but you don't have evidence to indicate it, do you?"

Gorman shook his head and said, "Unless he did it during one of those periods when we lost him."

"What about the night of the first two murders?"

"He was with Miss Foxworth."

"Where?"

"In his hotel room."

"Have you checked that with her?"

"One of my men saw them together, and if I did check it with her, she'd probably tell him."

"But he already knows you're following him."

"It's a game we're playing," Gorman said. "He pretends he doesn't know, and we pretend we're not following him."

"Maybe I should have a talk with Sweet."

"Are you friends?"

"Not friends," Clint said, standing up and stretching, "but we know each other."

"That might not be a bad idea, then," Gorman said, also

standing. "I can't condone it officially, mind you."

"I know that."

"But I can have a man go with you."

"Just keep your regular man watching him. There's no need to go to any bother on my account."

Clint checked the clock on the lieutenant's desk and saw that it was almost three in the morning.

"I'd better turn in. If I'm going to see Jeff Sweet, I want to be alert."

"Good idea. I can use some sleep myself."

"Going home?"

"No, I'll just curl up on a couch here." Gorman put his hand out and said, "Under the circumstances, it's been enjoyable."

Clint took the man's hand and said, "Does that mean I'm not a suspect anymore?"

"Everyone's a suspect," Gorman said, "but I'd say you were at the bottom of the list."

"Well," Clint said, moving toward the door, "that's one list I don't mind being at the bottom of."

# TWENTY-EIGHT

As Clint entered the lobby of his hotel, he saw the night clerk gesticulating furiously to attract his attention.

"What is it?" he asked, approaching the desk.

"I hope it's all right, Mr. Adams," the man said. "She said it would be."

"Who said what would be all right?"

"The woman, she said it would be all right if I let her into your room. She said she was a detective who was working with you on a case or something."

Amanda Foxworth.

"I hope it was all right," the man went on anxiously. "Was it all right?"

"Sure, it was all right. Don't worry about it."

The clerk beamed happily at having satisfied another hotel guest, and Clint mounted the steps to the second floor, wondering what was on Amanda's mind this time, business or sex.

He entered the room in no particular hurry, opening the door easily and half expecting to find her already in his bed.

She was in his bed, all right, but it wasn't Amanda Foxworth. It was Ellie Lennox.

"Hi," she said.

"Hi, yourself," he replied, closing the door behind him.

"I hope you don't mind."

"That depends on what you're here for, Ellie," he said. Her hair had a tousled look and she was very fetching, sitting there under the covers of his bed. "If all you're looking for is some companionship, I don't know if I'd have as much willpower this early in the morning as I did earlier. You look very lovely."

"I'm not looking for simple companionship, Clint," she said. "I'm looking for more."

With that she pushed the sheet away from her, showing herself to be naked.

She had an interesting body—interesting and lovely. Her breasts appeared to be very solid, round with hard, brown nipples, and in the valley between them were some light brown patches, almost like freckles, but larger. She kicked the sheet away and he could see that her thighs and calves were solid.

"Are you sure about this, Ellie?" he asked.

"I'm sure," she said, "and I want you to be sure, too."

"Oh, I'm sure," he said, starting to undress while she watched him. "I've been sure almost from the beginning."

"I was, too," she said. "I guess one of us should have said something."

"I guess so, but I think we were too busy fighting."

When he was as naked as she, he approached the bed and her hands reached eagerly for his engorged penis. She fondled it for a while and then continued with one hand while her other hand moved to his testicles. Beneath her touch, he felt himself grow as hard as a rock and fill almost to bursting. He reached for her breasts and began to return the favor, fondling her and finding her firm and smooth. Her nipples hardened even more and he tweaked each between his thumb and forefinger, causing her to catch her breath and close her eyes.

He moved to her, getting into bed next to her, momentarily breaking contact with her hands. When he was in bed with her, she grabbed hold of him again and began to pump her fist up and down the length of him. He reached behind her and cupped her buttocks, pulling her to him tightly, trapping her hand between them. When she freed her hand, she left one leg over his hip and he slid easily into her while they lay there side by side.

She started moving her hips slowly, a tempo he was content to match, letting her pull away from him gently and then pulling her back in with his hands on her buttocks. She began to moan and instinctively they both increased the tempo. At that point he rolled her over so that he was on top, and she reached for his buttocks with her hands and dug her nails into them as he drove into her. The tempo was all his now, and he increased it more and more until he was pounding into her relentlessly, bringing loud moans and cries from her. Soon they became words as she urged him on, telling him not to stop, to do it harder and faster. And then the words were blocked out as she cried out and climaxed, raking the skin of his butt with her nails. The pain from that seemed to send him off like a geyser and then he was moaning also as they came together.

Afterward they discussed the case, and Clint related everything that he and Gorman had talked about in the lieutenant's office.

"And you're going to see Sweet tomorrow?" she asked.

"Yes. Gorman said he's staying in a place called the American Hotel."

"I know where that is. I'll go with you."

"No, I think I'd better do this alone, Ellie. Sweet won't talk to me if you're around."

"I can come just to back you up."

"Don't worry," he said, "I'll tell you what Sweet says. We're partners, aren't we?"

"Yes," she said, "but that doesn't mean I trust you completely."

"What?" he said, sounding hurt.

"You might think you're trying to protect me, maybe because of what happened tonight. Okay, so I came apart a little bit. I admit it, but it won't happen again; I promise you that."

"I'm not worried about that, Ellie," he said. "I just want to make sure Sweet talks to me, and he might not with somebody else around."

"And that's all he'll do, talk? He won't try to kill you if it turns out he is the killer?"

"If he does try, I doubt that your presence there will affect the outcome," Clint said. "It would still be between him and me, and I'd have you to worry about. That would put me at a disadvantage."

Reluctantly she admitted that might be so. "But I'll hang around outside the hotel, just in case."

"You can do that," he agreed. "Maybe you can find Gorman's man and hang around together."

"Sure."

Clint didn't like the way that *sure* sounded, but he chose not to pursue it at the moment. There were other, more pleasurable pursuits available.

He leaned over her and began to run his tongue over those freckles between her breasts.

"Ugly, aren't they?"

"I think you've got marvelous breasts."

"I meant those brown spots. They look like stains, don't they?"

"They're marvelous, too," he assured her.

He continued to lick them until her nipples had hardened,

and then he switched his attention to the darker brown nubs. He scraped them with his teeth so that she shivered. Then he sucked on them until she moaned and wrapped her fingers in his hair.

"Oh, Clint . . ."

She pulled his head up so that she could kiss him, and during the kiss he maneuvered himself until he was between her legs, prodding her moist portal with the swollen head of his cock, teasing her.

But she wouldn't be teased. She brought her hips down so that she engulfed him, and then they began a happy, leisurely ride together that led to a mutually satisfying climax, after which they went to sleep in each other's arms.

# TWENTY-NINE

In the morning Clint went directly to the American Hotel, leaving Ellie behind in his room where he knew she wouldn't stay for long. He was surprised and pleased to find that there was no early morning awkwardness between them, and they made love one time before he left.

The American Hotel was a step down from the Denver House Hotel, but it was still one of the better hotels in town. Jeff Sweet must have been doing well financially in his chosen profession—unless his present client was footing the bill.

Clint found out the man's room number from the desk clerk and then, mounting the stairs, wondered idly if he'd find Amanda Foxworth in Sweet's room.

He knocked on the door and immediately heard the sound of footsteps approaching the door from the other side. They stopped and he heard the lock snap open. After several seconds the door still had not opened, and he knew that was going to be his job.

He turned the knob slowly, pushed the door inward so that it swung open, and then entered with his hands out in plain sight and empty.

"Clint Adams," Sweet said.

He was seated in a chair to Clint's right with a cocked .45 in his hand, putting the Gunsmith—or whoever his visitor might have turned out to be—at an immediate disadvantage.

"Hello, Sweet."

"Well, well . . ." Sweet said, letting his thoughts trail off, and he regarded the Gunsmith with a smile. "I'd say I had you at a disadvantage. I could put a bullet through your head right now, couldn't I?"

"You could," Clint said, "but you won't."

"Why not?"

"Two reasons," Clint said. "Number one, it's just not your style."

"And number two?"

"You want to know why I'm here."

Sweet hesitated a few seconds, then slipped the hammer on his gun down, and said, "You're right; I do. Come in and close the door."

Clint did so while Sweet stood up and put his gun back in his holster, which was hanging on the back of the chair he'd been sitting in.

Sweet was a tall man in his thirties, slender to the point of being frail, but Clint knew there was nothing frail about the man. He was deadly—with or without his gun—but his reputation had been built on the number of men he'd killed with his gun. He was supposed to be fast and accurate, traits Clint knew were rare in one man. One of those traits was usually good enough to keep a person alive for a while. Being accurate was the preferred talent, but for a man to be endowed with both . . .

"All right, so why are you here?" the professional killer asked.

"I'm sure you're aware of the murders that have occurred during the past week." If he killed them he was aware, and if he'd simply read about them in the newspapers, he was also aware.

"So?"

"I'm wondering if you have any connection with them, Jeff."

"Wonder away, Adams," Sweet said. "If I did, would I tell you?"

"I suppose not."

"Then tell me why you're really here."

"That's it."

"To ask me a question you knew I wouldn't answer?"

"And to watch your face while I asked it."

Sweet's face was thin. He had cheekbones that looked as if they wanted to burst from his face and cheeks that were great hollows. His mouth was a thin-lipped slit that seemed incapable of smiling, and his face, on the whole, rarely betrayed his inner feelings.

"And what did you see?"

"Nothing."

"Then you came for nothing."

"And got it."

The man's eyebrows came together in a frown, but it quickly vanished. It was the largest display of emotion Clint had ever seen from him, and it meant he was puzzled.

Good. That meant that the Gunsmith had gotten something after all.


"What did you get?" Ellie asked anxiously as Clint exited the hotel.

She offered no explanation why she was there because none was needed.

"I think I confused him."

"What did he say?"

''Nothing.''

''Did you come right out and ask him if he was involved with the killings?''

''Yes.''

''Wasn't that dangerous?''

''No. Whether he was or he wasn't, he wouldn't have answered.''

''Then why did you go to see him?''

''That's what he wanted to know, too.''

''And?''

''And I confused him, and that's why I went to see him. I knew I'd get nothing out of him, but I wanted him to see me.''

''You don't think he knew you were in town?''

''I don't know whether he did or not,'' Clint said, ''but I do now.''

They started across the street, and when they reached the other side and turned the corner, Ellie put her hand on Clint's arm and drew him back.

''What is it?'' he asked as she cautiously peered around the corner.

''Look.''

He looked in the direction she was indicating. Across the street, standing in a doorway a few doors away from the hotel, was Amanda Foxworth.

After Clint Adams left Jeff Sweet's room, there was a knock on his door. He knew who it was and answered it immediately.

''He just left,'' he said.

''I saw,'' the other man said. He had been waiting in a room down the hall for the Gunsmith to leave.

''What did he want?'' he asked, entering the room and closing the door behind him firmly.

"I'm not sure," Sweet said. "I think he just wanted to make sure I knew he was here."

"Why?"

"Maybe he thinks I'll make a try for him."

"And will you?"

"I might," Sweet said, "after our arrangement is finished."

"It's finished," the man said. He crossed to the window and looked out, spotting Clint Adams and Ellie Lennox crossing the street, well out of earshot.

"They're all dead," he said, turning to face Sweet, "all except one."

"And who's that?"

"You," the man said. He brought his hand out of his pocket. He was holding a little .32 revolver. Sweet's eyes widened and briefly he thought about his gun hanging on the back of the chair and the throwing knife—the one he'd used on the first two victims—in his boot.

He knew he'd never be able to reach them in time, and he didn't.

The gun made a surprisingly low popping noise as the man fired once. The bullet struck Sweet in the forehead, jerking his head back. His eyes rolled up and he fell over sideways. The sound he made striking the floor was louder than that of the shot, but the killer wasn't worried about that.

He wasn't worried about anything, anymore. He let himself out quickly, looked up and down the empty hallway, and walked to the stairs.

Down the stairs.

Out the door.

Free.

Now they were all dead, the man thought as he left the hotel. Dorothy Chandler and her husband, Evelyn McCloud, Vincent Thurston, and the last person who could have tied him to the whole thing, Jeff Sweet. It had been Sweet who killed all the others, but it was his employer who was actually the killer, a man who had wanted all of those people dead for his own reasons.

And for someone else's.

# THIRTY

Only the killer had made a mistake. There was still one more person who could tie him to everything, and he found her waiting for him when he got home. The gun in her hand was very much like the one in his pocket and very unlike the one he was wearing under his arm in a shoulder rig.

"How'd you get in here?"

"I bribed the desk clerk."

"What do you want?"

"I followed you."

"When?"

"Just now, and then I rushed back here to get here before you."

"So?"

"I know."

"You know what?"

"I know that you've been behind all the killings."

"Is that a fact?"

"What I don't know is why."

"Is that important?"

"Probably not—not to me, anyway, but the police will probably ask you."

"The police? Have you sent for them?"

"No, I want to bring you in myself."

"Do you think you can?"

"If I didn't think I could, I wouldn't be here."

"It'll be quite a feather in your cap with the old man, won't it?"

"With everyone."

"What made you suspect me?"

"You were never around, and I found that suspicious. Also, Sweet talked to me when we were in bed."

"You and Sweet?"

"Does that surprise you? It shouldn't. He's not handsome, not like you, but he's very attractive, and he's very good in bed—unlike you."

"You're trying to make me angry."

"No, I'm not. You're trying to keep me talking for some reason. Don't tell me you have an accomplice?"

"No accomplice."

"Well, there's got to be someone else. You don't have a motive for any of these killings that I can see."

"I thought you weren't interested in why?"

"I'm not. Take your gun out of your shoulder holster and put it down on the floor."

"Amanda, you wouldn't shoot me."

"Sure I would. Remember what you said about a feather in my cap? I wouldn't let you take that away from me. I wouldn't let anyone take that away from me."

"You and Sweet, I can't figure that."

"The gun!"

"He's dead, you know."

"What?"

"Sweet's dead. I killed him."

"You couldn't have."

"I did. Bang, one right in the forehead. It was easy because he wasn't expecting it."

"You—"

"Still want my gun?"

He swept back his coat in order to get at the gun and brought out a large .45, holding it in front of him by the barrel.

"Drop it."

"It might go off."

"Lay it down."

"Come and take it."

Indecision was her undoing. This was not a situation she was accustomed to dealing with. She took a tentative step forward, as if she were going to take the gun, and then he said, "Catch!" and tossed it to her.

She moved to catch the heavy weapon, momentarily forgetting the one in her hand. The man's other hand came out of his pocket holding the .32, and he fired once.

In the hallway outside Clint and Ellie were puzzling over this recent turn of events.

"Why would she be following him?" Ellie asked, frowning. "They're supposed to be working together. If I had known where she was going I wouldn't have suggested following her." She allowed her statement to trail off, her disappointment plain on her face and in her tone.

"Maybe they haven't been working well together," Clint suggested. "Maybe he's been going out on his own, so she decided to follow him. It was just a coincidence that we were all in the same place at the same time."

"Do you think he was there to see Sweet?"

"Why else?"

"Where was he while you were up there?"

"He must have gotten there ahead of me," Clint said, "and he was waiting somewhere until I left."

"Why?"

"That's a good question. Unless . . ."

"Unless what?"

He looked at her and said, "Unless they were working together—"

He didn't get a chance to finish his statement because they heard a sharp popping sound from behind the closed door, followed by a couple of thudding sounds.

"Gunshot?" she asked.

"Small caliber," he said, nodding. "Let's go."

They moved to the door, and as Ellie was about to knock, Clint swept her out of the way and kicked the door open.

Inside Ken Sapir was leaning over the prone figure of Amanda Foxworth. The front of Amanda's shirt showed a red hole that was oozing. Sapir stared at them, a small caliber revolver in one hand and a .45 in the other.

"What's going on—" Ellie started to demand, but Sapir brought both guns to bear on them and her statement was cut off. Once again, Clint Adams swept her out of the way, only this time with more force.

As he pushed her, Clint jumped away from her and to the other side of the doorway, just as Sapir's .45 went off. The Pinkerton-gone-bad backed away toward the window against the far wall, holding both guns ahead of him.

"Sapir—" Clint began to say.

The man kept moving.

"You'll never make it."

"Ken—" Ellie called out, struggling to her feet with a .32 in her hand.

"Ellie, no!" Clint shouted.

He had wanted Sapir alive, but Ellie's move had taken that decision out of his hands. She was bringing her gun up, but he saw that Sapir was going to beat her easily. As he pointed the .45 at her, Clint drew and fired. His bullet struck Sapir in the chest. The impact drove him back. He struck the window with all his weight, shattering it and falling through it in a blinding, winking shower of glass.

"Shit!" Clint said with feeling. He rushed to the window to look out. From the way the body was lying on the ground, it was obvious to Clint that Ken Sapir was dead.

# THIRTY-ONE

Early the following day Clint Adams, Ellie Lennox, and Lieutenant Gorman visited Senator Alvin McCloud at his home.

"Did you find out who killed Thurston?" McCloud asked Gorman when they were all assembled in his office.

"Senator, I'm going to let Mr. Adams conduct this interview since he and Miss Lennox did all the work on this."

"Interview?" McCloud said, looking at Clint.

"Well, it's not an interview really," he said. "What's happened is that Miss Lennox and I have formed some theories, and we want to get your reaction to them."

"Well, I did ask you to keep me apprised of your progress. All right," he said, sitting back in his chair, "go ahead and theorize."

"All right," Clint said, "now I want you to understand the entire basis of this theory is that you had your wife murdered."

"What?" The senator sat straight up in his chair as if struck by lightning. "What the hell are you talking about?"

"Let's count the dead," Clint went on. "Your wife, the Chandlers—killed separately, of course—and Vincent Thurston, all killed by a man named Jeff Sweet."

"I don't know any Jeff Sweet."

"We know that," Clint said, "but you knew Kenneth Sapir?"

"Sapir?"

"A Pinkerton who has done some work for you from time to time—meaningless things, mostly—that is, until now."

"Sapir," McCloud said, as if trying to recall the name. "He was working on my wife's murder, wasn't he?"

"That's right?"

"Wait, you said I *knew* him?"

"Sapir is dead, too," Clint continued, "killed by me after he killed Jeff Sweet and another Pinkerton agent named Amanda Foxworth."

"She was his partner!"

"Right."

"They're dead? That's unfortunate—"

"They're all dead, so that none of what I'm about to say can be proven—unless, of course, you decide to confess."

"To what?"

"To instigating what eventually led to the death of seven people, all to further your political career."

"This is beginning to sound—"

"Let me go on," Clint said, cutting him off, and McCloud sat back with a disgusted expression on his face.

"I think—"

"We think," Ellie Lennox said.

"Right," Clint said, "excuse me. We think that you were not so unaffected by your wife's infidelity as you would have us believe. In fact, we think it bothered you quite a bit, so much so that you went to Dorothy Chandler and told her about it. Now, even though both of your egos were hurt, you found yourselves attracted to each other and started an affair of your own, all the while plotting to get even with your spouses. Finally, you decided to murder them."

"That's ridiculous. I wouldn't endanger my career—"

"Sympathy," Clint said, cutting him off again. "You've said it yourself so many times. The sympathy vote is just as good as any other, and you didn't want the news of your cuckolding getting out some other way, because that would make you look like a fool. This way your wife was murdered, and incidentally, she was having an affair. Poor Senator McCloud."

"Lieutenant—" McCloud said.

"I found all of this quite interesting," Gorman said. "I think you will, too."

"You needed someone to kill them for you, but you didn't have those contacts, so you got in touch with someone who did."

"Who?"

"A Pinkerton agent named Kenneth Sapir."

"Why would he do such a thing?"

"For money, money paid to him by you and supplied by you and Dorothy Chandler together, so that neither one of you had to pay the freight alone. So, Sapir gets Sweet to come to town to kill your wife and Dorothy's husband, only while he's here Dorothy gets a look at him and it's bye-bye senator."

"*I* called that relationship off myself!"

"That's not the point."

"Then what is?"

"You were no longer sleeping together, but you were still co-conspirators in murder. You started to get nervous—and maybe a little jealous—so you decided to put Dorothy out of the way where she couldn't hurt you."

"And who killed her?"

"Jeff Sweet."

"You just said he was sleeping with her."

"Jeff Sweet was a professional killer," Clint said. "He'd

just as soon kill a woman as sleep with her. That was no problem, and again you arranged it with Sapir. Sweet had no idea he was working for you.''

''Why did I have Thurston killed?''

''You understand we'll never know the true answers to all of this unless you confess,'' Clint said, ''but I guess that he started to suspect something, and through Sapir, you had him killed.''

''So I'm a homicidal maniac now?''

''No, not you,'' Clint said, ''that title goes to Jeff Sweet. He got caught up in this epidemic of murder. You see, Ken Sapir killed Sweet to get him out of the way and then he was going to blackmail you.''

''What?''

''He had a huge file on the murders, and although there's nothing concrete in it for the police to act on, there's enough to form a theory—as I've just done.''

''And now Sapir's dead?''

''And Miss Foxworth, who became suspicious of her partner who was never around when she wanted him, and so she followed him—and died trying to bring him in.''

Clint stopped talking, and after a moment, McCloud said, ''Is that it?''

''That's it.''

''Lieutenant, are you prepared to arrest me for murder or conspiracy to commit murder?''

''No, sir, I'm not.''

''Then I suggest that you all leave.''

''Are you prepared to confess to these crimes, sir?'' the lieutenant asked.

''I most certainly am not.''

McCloud saw the lieutenant look at Clint Adams, who nodded, and then Gorman said to McCloud, ''Then I have no choice but to arrest you.''

"For what?"

Gorman stepped forward and slapped a handcuff on the man's right wrist before the senator realized what was happening.

"Owen McClain, I arrest you on the charge of conspiracy to commit fraud against the state and against the government of the United States. Mr. Adams has provided a complete folder of your past activities."

McClain looked at Clint angrily, and the Gunsmith said, "You didn't leave me any choice, Owen."

McClain was about to reply when Gorman snapped the other handcuff tight over his left wrist, causing him to wince in pain.

"And you know what?" Clint continued. "I think that last charge should bring you just as much time as if you'd been convicted of murder."

# THIRTY-TWO

"Seven people," Ellie Lennox said. "That's incredible—and what's even more frightening is that the man might have become President of the United States."

Clint and Ellie were in the dining room of the Denver House Hotel. Two days had passed since the arrest of Owen McClain—that was the only name he was known by now, his true name—and they had spent much of those two days together, getting to know each other as people and not as partners.

"We stopped him, Ellie," Clint said. "That's all that matters."

"I guess so."

"What did Pinkerton have to say about this?" Clint asked. He had not seen Pinkerton since the arrest and had no desire to. "I'll bet he's proud of you."

"I told him it was mostly Amanda's doing."

"You did?"

"Well, it was," she said, looking up from her plate at him. "If it hadn't been for Amanda leading us to Ken Sapir, we'd still be looking for the killer."

"That was nice of you to point out."

"She did the job and she died for it," Ellie said. "The least

I can do is make sure she gets the credit—for all the good it will do her now.''

''What did Pinkerton say?''

''He said there would definitely be more serious work for me after this.''

''I guess he figures you must have deserved some credit, too.''

''As a matter of fact,'' she said, digging into her bag, ''I'm supposed to leave for California today.'' She showed him her train ticket. ''Seems they need a Pinkerton out there, and Mr. Pinkerton said he thought I was right for the job.''

Clint reached across the table and took her hand.

''That's great, Ellie.''

''Yeah.''

''That's what you want, isn't it? To be taken serious, to be given real cases to work on?''

''I suppose—yes, that's what I want, all right.''

''Then what's wrong?''

''I guess I'm wondering if I'm really cut out for this kind of work. I mean, I can't stop thinking of those seven people. All right, maybe Sweet and Sapir deserved to die, but the others didn't. They hadn't done anything so horrible that they had to die for it.''

''If you weren't thinking about them,'' Clint said, ''then I'd be worried about you, but now I'm not. You're going to be just fine.''

She squeezed his hand back and said, ''Well, what about you?''

''What about me?''

''Where will you go from here?''

''I don't know.''

''Will I ever see you again.''

''Honey, I don't know that either.''

''We wasted a lot of time arguing, didn't we?''

"We wasted some," he said, "but we made up for it some over the past couple of days."

"Yes, we did, didn't we?"

They stared at each other across the table and then Clint said, "I've still got some time before my train leaves."

"So have I."

"Want to make up for it some more? I haven't checked out of my room yet."

Grinning from ear to ear, she said, "I thought you'd never ask."

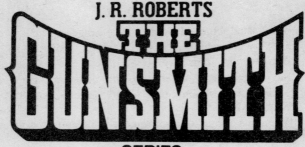

# J. R. ROBERTS
# THE GUNSMITH

## SERIES

Prices may be slightly higher in Canada.

*Available at your local bookstore or return this form to:*

 **CHARTER**
*THE BERKLEY PUBLISHING GROUP, Dept. B*
*390 Murray Hill Parkway, East Rutherford, NJ 07073*

Please send me the titles checked above. I enclose _____ Include $1.00 for postage and handling if one book is ordered; 25¢ per book for two or more not to exceed $1.75. California, Illinois, New Jersey and Tennessee residents please add sales tax. Prices subject to change without notice and may be higher in Canada.

NAME_____

ADDRESS_____

CITY_____ STATE/ZIP_____

(Allow six weeks for delivery.)

A1/a